I0764486

Postcards

Other Books by Timothy Glass

Non-Fiction

Just This Side of Heaven

Children
(Sleepytown Beagles Series)

Sleepytown Beagles: Differences
Sleepytown Beagles: Oh, Brother
Sleepytown Beagles: Penny's 4th of July
Sleepytown Beagles: Panda Meets Ms. Daisy Bloom

Postcards

T. Faron

Postcards
Timothy Glass writing as T. Faron

This book is a work of fiction. Names, characters, places, and incidents are the product of the author's imagination and are used fictitiously. Any resemblance or similarity to actual events, locations, or individuals, living or deceased, is purely coincidental. The work is from the author's imagination.

Cover and Interior Design by Daniel Middleton
www.scribefreelance.com

Platinum Paw Press
Visit our website www.platinumpawpress.com

Library of Congress Control Number: 2009901201

ISBN: 978-0-9984121-5-3

Printed in the Untied State of America

To Betty, because you are a wonderful inspiration to everyone who has ever had the pleasure to know you. You are amazing in every sense of the word.

Acknowledgments

As always, no book would be complete without mentioning my wife, Cathy. Your understanding and support of my long hours of research and writing makes this all possible. You are my one!

To my honorary mom, Lynn, for her continued motivation.

To our service men and women who serve and protect our country and our freedom.

Thank you to all the fellow journalists who gave up their time to help me with this project. I give special thanks to Simon Robinson, *Time* magazine, and Charles Jones, author of *Red, White, or Yellow* for sharing their experiences gained from reporting in Iraq. Both of you have helped breathe life and added depth to my character. For this, I will always be eternally grateful.

To P.T. Gray, one of my many mentors, thank you for sharing your gift of knowledge and following my career for all these years.

To Daniel, my editor, may you know how much you are appreciated.

For Everyone, There
is That ♡ne…

Chapter One

SARA KETCHAM OVERLAPPED the fabric of her jacket, pulling the left side over the right as she drew it closer to her slender body. But since that was hardly enough, she then crossed her arms over her chest and tucked her hands under her arms to keep them warm, and to ward off the chill of the ocean breeze. September evenings were often chilly here at Brant Rock, located just outside Marshfield, Massachusetts, but Sara had never liked the cold, even after living in New England all of her life. She only braved it now for the sake of the stunning views the beach provided.

The rhythmic sound of the ocean's tide was almost hypnotic as the white foam bubbled onto the sandy beach and disappeared, slowly rolling back out to sea. Off in the distance, seagulls playfully called to one another. The beach was almost deserted at this hour in the evening, and only impressions of footprints remained in the sand as a reminder of the visitors who walked here today. Puffy clouds hung overhead and loomed large, and as the sun set in the western sky, offering the last glow of afternoon light, the clouds appeared to be illuminated from behind like a photographer's light box.

Sara slowly strolled beside the water's edge, while Molly, her three-year-old tri-colored beagle, launched playfully toward a gull, baying as the bird took off in flight. Sara closed her eyes as if magically allowing her mind to drift back in time. When she was a little girl, she would play for hours here at Brant Rock beach. She could almost smell the sweet aroma of her grandmother's snickerdoodle cookies as they cooled on the baking racks near the open kitchen window.

Those were happier, more carefree times. Sara would spend hours building sandcastles by day in the warm summer sunshine. The only worry she had back then was when that darn freckle-faced Franklin boy who lived three doors down from her grandmother's would wander down to the beach. After sneaking up from the side, he would kick the walls of her sandcastle in. And the madder she got, the more he would laugh at her.

Sara opened her eyes and found that she stood not more than five feet away from a sandcastle that lay in ruins on the beach before her. Tears rolled down her cheeks as she bent down and began to fix it. The sandcastle was representative of her life today, only her life and home had been torn apart by a man she vowed to love forever. The problem was that her forever and Russ' forever were not the same. Just like the mean little freckle-faced Franklin boy, Russ had managed to tear apart everything they had built up together through the course of their 12-year marriage.

Sara had worked both day and night while Russ finished up his MBA at Harvard Business School. Russ was destined for success. She reminded him of this each time he wanted to give up and quit. Now, Russ was a successful financial planner who wore business suits that cost more than the rent on their old studio apartment. His days were spent in a high-rise office building on Congress Street that overlooked downtown Boston's financial district. As Russ climbed the ladder of success, he managed to leave Sara and Molly behind. Russ exchanged forever for a woman ten years younger than him.

It had been eight months, and the divorce papers still lay signed and sealed in an envelope on her dresser back in Norwood. It was as if touching them after their divorce was finalized would make them real. She found herself wondering how Russ could do this to her. She could overlook a lot of things, and had done so in her lifetime—her mother always said she had the patience of Job—but a marriage was based on trust, and that was something Russ had managed to destroy. When all was said and done, and despite her patience, she felt betrayed and deceived by the very man she loved.

They were always going to start planning a family. Nevertheless, each time she mentioned the subject, Russ managed to change it. Given the outcome, she was thankful there were no children to be hurt by their failed marriage. God knows how much she was pained by their breakup, and poor Molly was still hurting. Molly had an internal clock; she knew when Russ was due to come home from work. She would lie down by the back door waiting for Russ to return home each evening at 5:45. When Sara found her faithfully waiting by the door, it broke her heart. Many evenings, she would sit on the floor beside Molly and pull her close to her and cry for them both. As Sara's intense crying shook both their bodies, that was Molly's cue to sit up and look deep into Sara's eyes as if to comfort her.

Their friends were torn by their breakup, too. She suddenly found herself no longer part of a couple at family outings and get-togethers. Friends and family attempted to ignore the fact that she was the only single person in the group. But, the harder they tried, the more she felt out of place. Her solution to this was to make up excuses when asked to attend get-togethers.

Jane was the one friend who would not take no for an answer from Sara. They had met at a fundraiser for a local animal shelter and had been close friends ever since. While she understood Sara's feelings about group settings, Jane made it a point to meet her for lunch. Even so, no matter what the two talked about, the subject would always manage to gravitate back to Russ.

The trip to Brant Rock would be different, she assured herself. She needed time away; away from the house she and Russ had shared for years, and before the start of the new school year at that. God knows, for months her thoughts had been nothing more than fragments within her mind. This trip would help her sort out those fragments by putting all those puzzle pieces together. Nevertheless, the sight of the sandcastle brought her to tears.

Chapter Two

RYAN SPENCER PEERED out of the airplane window as the aircraft banked left toward the runway and the "Fasten Seat Belt" light illuminated overhead. He noticed that the sky surrounding Boston's Logan airport was a grayish blue. Since they were coming in for a landing, the plane's airspeed slowed significantly and created a wonderful sensation that caused the passengers to feel as though they were floating over the city. Ryan quickly turned off his computer and slipped it, along with a stack of paperwork, into his briefcase. He was no stranger to business travel. His life was always centered around his next business trip. He stowed his briefcase under the seat in front of him and took a glance around the plane at the nameless sea of faces of the passengers sharing the flight. He wondered if they had someone waiting for them at Logan. He secretly missed that in his life. Nonetheless, it had been a long time since someone awaited his arrival anywhere.

His lifestyle today resembled that of a nomad. He had traveled for the last eighteen months and lived primarily out of a suitcase. The house he and his wife called home for years was gone. Moreover, most everything else was sold or given away—a causality of divorce.

After the divorce, he reasoned with himself, thinking, *What do I need with a house? After all, being single and traveling all the time doesn't lend itself well to being a homeowner.* In fact, that was the reason Ann had left him for another man. At least that's what she told him. He had been through this a million times in his mind. What if he had known? If only she had said that his work had bothered her. Instead, he came home and found her in the arms of another man. Gone was the life that they had shared, and soon after, the separation had claimed everything that went with it. It wasn't that he was unwilling to work on their marriage; he simply hadn't known how discontented Ann had become. A part of Ann wanted to work on it, too. However, no matter how hard she had tried, the fact was she was in love with another man. Ryan had asked her to stay, telling her he was willing to give up his career and the constant traveling associated with it. Nonetheless, the damage was done; the marriage was over.

Six months after the divorce was final, the house was sold to a young couple. Ryan packed the clothes and belongings he needed for his next assignment. After tossing them into a rental car, he left the rest of his possessions on the curb for charity to pick up. The memory of those images from the rear view mirror was all he had left.

That image both haunted him and drove him to push harder. He became engrossed in his work, volunteering for more and more assignments. The farther away, the better. Each time his work was completed he would pick a place—any place—to stay. Just like the job, it really did not matter where. This time he picked a small coastal town in New England in which to rest up before his next assignment.

After the plane touched down, Ryan grabbed his briefcase and duffle bag, then caught the rental car shuttle. A young married couple sat across from him, holding hands. The young man pointed out the bus window as he whispered something to his wife, and she offered a sweet smile in response to whatever he had told her. No matter where or how far Ryan traveled, he always encountered people who were either in love or in the midst of expressing love to one another. Despite his efforts to avoid these people and their open displays of affection, he found himself coming face-to-face with them over and over again.

He tried to put the thought out of his mind as he tossed his duffle bag into the back seat of the rental car. After climbing behind the wheel, he headed south of Boston on route 95.

Chapter Three

THE SOUND OF MOLLY'S bark startled Sara. While it was a playful bark, and not one of alarm, Sara glanced up.

"Molly!" She shouted, suddenly noticing a man playing with her beagle.

Molly ran toward her as the man followed behind. Sara felt embarrassed and vulnerable as she quickly wiped the tears from her eyes. She realized that he was the man from yesterday, who had checked into the bed and breakfast where she was staying. His smile was the first thing that caught her attention, particularly the way it made his dimples appear. As they passed each other, she turned and took a second glance. She remembered that he looked out of place staying at an inn on the beach. For one thing, he had worn cowboy boots, a nicely pressed white shirt that was neatly tucked into a pair of snug-fitting Wrangler jeans, and he carried a briefcase. Put together, it all seemed odd; yet there was something about his appearance that struck her as refreshingly different. She remembered laughing to herself as she opened the front door to leave the inn, when she overheard him say "y'all" to the innkeeper.

"Molly, I told you not to wander off," Sara said, firmly.

"Molly? Is that your name?" The stranger bent down to pet Molly. Then he stood up, smiled, and said, "Hi, my name is Ryan." He moved in closer, extended his hand toward Sara and noticed her puffy eyes and tear-stained cheeks, and the ruined sandcastle at her feet.

"You okay?" he asked.

Realizing that he was staring at her teary eyes, she quickly rubbed them dry and said, "Allergies. Love the beach . . . hate the sand." Sara sniffled to drive her point home.

"Me too," he said, furrowing his brow as he took a backward glance at the long stretch of beach. "I've never done well around sand either."

"No boots today."

"Boots? Oh, you're the lady from the inn yesterday."

"That was me and Molly."

"No, I thought the sandals would be more stylish. What d'ya think?" Ryan took a step back, both arms extended, and turned in a circle as he modeled his wardrobe.

Sara laughed. She couldn't help but notice how muscled and tanned his legs were as they extended from the pair of khaki cargo shorts he wore.

"Definitely more stylish," Sara said, feeling herself blush.

"Let me help." Ryan bent down to the sandcastle and began restoring one of the walls.

"So, I know you build sandcastles for a living and your beagle's name is Molly. Do you have a name?"

"Sara—Sara Ketcham. I'm a third grade teacher. Molly and I only build sandcastles part-time." Sara smiled at her own joke as her eyes were drawn to his infectious smile. It was those darn dimples, she was sure of it.

"And you? You break horses for a living, I presume?"

Confused at first by her assumption, he said nothing while looking at her with a blank expression on his face.

"Your boots. Yesterday you had on boots."

"Oh," he said chuckling, noticing how pretty her dark eyes were. "No, my dad was a cattle rancher."

"Your dad has a cattle ranch here in Massachusetts?"

"No. Actually, he passed away from a stroke a few years back."

"I'm sorry," Sara said, bending down to help. She watched him repair the sandcastle wall with a deft and gentle movement of his hands. "Is poor mom back there on the ranch, all by herself?"

Ryan hesitated for a few seconds. "No, she passed away, too."

Sara noticed the sadness in Ryan's eyes when he mentioned his father's passing; however, when he told her about his mother, his eyes moistened and for a moment he turned away. Sara was suddenly uncomfortable. She never felt as though she knew the right thing to say, and certainly not with a perfect stranger. She was always amazed by people who could strike up a conversation with a perfect stranger on the subway or in a café, but she was simply just not that way.

Wanting to end the conversation, she took a nervous glance at her watch, and said, "God, look at the time. We'd better be going. I have to get Molly her dinner."

Ryan rose to his feet and took her hand to help her up.

As he patted Molly on the head, he said, "It was nice meeting you both. Enjoy your stay."

Sara began walking toward the inn, and Ryan watched as Molly playfully scampered alongside her.

Chapter Four

SARA FILLED THE claw-footed porcelain tub with warm water and some bubble bath, and lit two candles. After walking across the room, she switched the bedside radio on and channel-surfed until she found some soft jazz playing. She was glad she had stopped by the old general store on her way back to the inn to pick up a bottle of White Zinfandel. She poured herself a glass of the chilled wine and carefully placed it next to the candles.

After removing her clothes, she passed by the antique oval mirror that hung on the wall and glanced at her own reflection for a moment. At thirty-two, her body was still firm and trim, which she attributed to her and Molly's daily walks before work—not to mention her job as a third grade teacher; the children themselves provided a good workout, being the tightly wound balls of energy they were at that age.

Satisfied with the reflection in the mirror, she then made her way to the inviting tub and carefully climbed in—seeing the water was piping hot—and began to take a relaxing soak beneath a mound of suds. After taking a sip of wine, she leaned her head back and watched the candlelight cast shadowy patterns that danced on the ceiling above her, in perfect tune with the music emanating softly from the radio in the bedroom. Molly curled up on the bathmat in front of the tub. Sara found herself thinking about her day. Nonetheless, her mind drifted back to Ryan and the time they had spent together on the beach that evening. She wondered why she was even giving him a second thought. It was foolish of her; he was probably just being polite. Having closed her eyes, she felt every muscle in her body relax as she took another sip of wine and exhaled. No matter how hard she tried not to, somehow her mind kept returning to Ryan.

He was shorter than Russ; probably around five-foot nine or so, she guessed. He looked close to her age—early thirties. His body looked like someone who made daily trips to the gym. He had dark brown hair . . . hazel eyes. . . .

"Wait just a minute, buddy," Sara said, as she slid upward into a sitting position. She had done it so abruptly that the bathtub water swished back and forth, causing Molly to stand up and gaze intently at her—on top of that, she was talking to herself. Molly playfully wagged her tail in response to what she was witnessing.

"Oh, he is slick, Molly—Slick, I tell you! Did you notice how he avoided telling me where he was from? Mr. Cattle Rancher with the dimples. Hmmph!"

Sara slowly slid back down against the back of the tub, deep in thought.

After a moment of that, she said, "I'll just bet he has a wife and a handful of kids somewhere. You'll notice I told him what I do for a living, but did he . . . really?" Sara looked at Molly. Molly wagged her tail and tilted her head from side to side, as though she was listening to Sara's every word.

"Oh, I know you were probably taken in by those dimples, too, weren't you, girl?"

Molly gave a quick, playful bark.

"We'll just make sure that if we run into Mr. Cattle Rancher with the dimples tomorrow, that we get some real answers. Right, Molly girl?" Sara reached out a hand and patted Molly, depositing a few soap bubbles on top of her head. As Sara leaned her head back, she suddenly realized how untrusting she sounded to herself. She shook her head in disapproval of her own behavior.

"God, I'm starting to sound like my mother now."

Guilt washed over her like the warm water in the tub. She began to reason with herself. Ryan was just a guy she had met on the beach. *For heaven's sake*, she told herself, *it's not like I'm interested in him.*

Chapter Five

BACK AT THE INN, Ryan kicked off his sandals and climbed onto the four-poster bed. The old bed was inviting, with more than the usual number of fluffy pillows, which reminded him of the time he was a kid living at his parents' house. As he leaned back against the pillows he remembered Sara's question about his family, and how much he missed his parents, especially his mom. It wasn't that he didn't love his father, it's just that his mother had been his best friend, and they had always shared a special bond. He sat up and glanced out the window. It was quiet and peaceful outside. From this viewpoint, it was almost like watching a silent movie as he sat and observed the ocean waves gracefully roll toward the shoreline and back out to sea.

Ryan felt relaxed in this quaint coastal town. Brant Rock was far removed from his normal daily lifestyle and routine. This, he reasoned within himself, was just what he needed—quiet downtime to escape the death and destruction he had seen over the last few months. Meeting Sara was something he had not counted on. She intrigued him. After his divorce, friends had tried to play the matchmaking game with him, but invariably failed. Ryan was simply not a willing participant. He was still emotionally exhausted months after his divorce from Ann.

Sara, though their meeting was casual and brief, seemed different from other women. Theirs had been a chance encounter on the beach. He would be leaving in two weeks on another assignment, far away from Brant Rock. Distance had a way of preventing relationships from developing. Over the last eighteen months he had learned to distance himself from almost everything, except his work, and the long hours it demanded of him. But the bloodshed was behind him for now. All he needed tonight was a hot meal and a good night's sleep.

Chapter Six

THE SUN POKED ITS lazy head up over the Atlantic Ocean. Sara stood and gazed at it through a veil of fog that hung over the shore. She shivered in the morning chill and resumed her stroll along the beach. At this hour in the morning she found the tranquil setting quite refreshing. She closed her eyes, took a few deep breaths, and exhaled. She could taste the sea salt on her lips and feel the mist in the air. The breeze was light off the ocean, but strong enough to lift her dark brown hair slightly from her shoulders.

The morning was perfect. Molly bounded ahead of Sara, chasing the seagulls into flight out over the ocean. Sara found a spot in the sand where she could sit and face the water. As she did so, she watched the waves roll within inches of her feet, then swirl back into the sea, etching patterns in the sand as they receded. It was as if the sand that lay before her was the ocean's own personal canvas, painting a new portrait with each successive wave. She reminded herself that this was the very reason she had come to Brant Rock in the first place. It was this peaceful existence her body, mind, and soul needed.

Glancing at her watch, she knew that Russ would be heading for the station right about now to catch the commuter train into Boston on his way to work. The thought pained her at first; nevertheless, she was finally realizing that they were now going in different directions with their lives. There was no turning back; she just had to accept the hand of cards life had dealt her. While she knew it would be hard getting by on the East Coast with one income, deep down she thought she could do it—or at least give it her best shot.

The divorce settlement had awarded her the three-bedroom colonial style house she and Russ had purchased five years ago, but along with it came the mortgage and insurance payments. Russ had left everything behind for his new life. She considered for a moment whether she had made Russ' leaving all too easy. However, it made no sense to hold him to a commitment made years ago when, in reality, he was already gone by the time she had found out about the other woman.

At the time she thought it was simply a phase they were going through. Her mother always told her that God never closed a door unless he opened another. *What really does that mean in my situation?* she thought now. *Will there be another chance at love—and will I recognize this new doorway in my life? How will I even know what door to open?*

She sat, staring beyond the waves that rolled upon the ocean canvas before her, and in that moment she knew she must find the strength within her heart to let go and move forward. She quickly wiped away a tear as it rolled down her cheek. Molly ran to her side when she stood up and removed her wedding band from the pocket of her faded jeans. Looking at the band of gold in the palm of her hand, the memories came rushing back, and she clearly remembered the day Russ had placed it on her finger. . . .

THE WEATHER WAS PERFECT for an outdoor New England wedding in June. There was not a cloud in sight amidst the canopy of blue above. Her mother had stressed for weeks over the weather and the idea of an outdoor wedding, and she had asked Sara repeatedly, "Shouldn't you at the very least have a backup plan?" However, this is what Sara and Russ had wanted: a seaside, June, New England wedding.

White chairs formed a circle around the bride and groom. She and Russ had come up with the idea during their search for the perfect place to hold the event.

"Weddings always start out with family and friends divided," Sara told Russ, holding his hand tightly as they considered the merits of the hotel garden for their special day. She added, "We could put the chairs in a circle. This way, everyone would be sitting together."

On the day of the wedding, Sara's father escorted her slowly toward the center of the circle where Russ was waiting for her. He was extremely handsome in his midnight black tuxedo. Sara could see her mother already dabbing tears from her eyes as she caught sight of her and her father. . . .

NONETHELESS, THAT WAS then and this was now. No amount of planning could have prepared her for the outcome. The end result was that she and Russ were no longer married. With the ring clenched in one hand, Sara slipped off her sandals and rolled her pant legs up above her knees. Her first step into the chilly water took her breath away. Having caught it, she walked out into the expansive ocean. She looked at the gold band one last time, blinked back tears, and tossed the ring as far out into the ocean as she could. The ring landed on the crest of a small wave and bobbed up and down for a few seconds before disappearing from her sight. Molly thought this was a game of fetch and began to splash out into the ocean after the wedding band.

"Molly, no!" Sara commanded, which immediately brought the dog back to her side. She bent down and petted Molly. "Hopefully, a little girl will find it someday and think she's found a real treasure. What d'ya think, Molly girl?"

Molly seemed to understand, given the way she tilted her head from side to side as she listened intently to Sara's every word.

Chapter Seven

SARA STOOD MOTIONLESS, watching the ocean swells churn before her. There was just a hint of white caps forming at the top of the waves. She clasped her hands together to warm them from the cold Atlantic breezes blowing off the ocean. She had been so deep in thought she didn't even realize she had begun to inch backward until her body bumped into something.

"Oh, God!" she blurted, startled. She gasped and quickly spun around to see what she had run into.

"Sorry. I just came over the dune for a walk and saw you and Molly here on the beach. I didn't mean to frighten you." Ryan grasped Sara's shoulders to steady her.

Sara caught her breath and said, "I didn't hear you come up behind me," then her hand went to her chest.

Ryan watched her hand rising and falling with each rapid beat of her heart. He glanced up at her face next and noticed that her dark brown eyes were puffy and red.

"Join me?" Ryan said to her, as he leaned down

to pet Molly on the head. "For a morning walk, I mean."

"Ah—really, I should be . . ." Before she could finish her sentence, Molly barked playfully and wagged her tail while looking up at Ryan.

"Well, I'll take that as a yes. See? Molly thinks it's a great idea. Right, Molly?" Molly let out another playful bark as Ryan patted her head again.

Sara shook her head and gave a resounding sigh. "You're incorrigible."

"Me?" Ryan said, as he stood up.

"Actually, I was talking about Molly, but I think the two of you are fast becoming partners in crime."

Molly scampered playfully around Ryan's legs while looking up at him. Sara could see that Molly was thrilled to be with Ryan, and she noticed how lively and animated she would become whenever Ryan would show up. But despite that, Sara knew in her heart that Molly still missed Russ.

Ryan posed his question again. "What d'ya say? Up for a walk?"

Sara shook her head in disbelief at his persistence.

"Say 'Yes, Ryan, I would love to take a beautiful morning stroll along the beach with you,'" he prompted, noticing her hesitation.

Sara couldn't help but smile at Ryan as she

nodded. "Okay, you two. I guess I'm outvoted here."

Sara and Ryan began their walk along the water's edge, side by side. Molly trotted a few feet ahead of them, wagging her tail, but she turned back to check on them every few feet.

Ryan decided to break the silence first. "She is a beautiful beagle. I love her personality."

"Did you have a dog on the ranch?" Sara asked, as she looked over at him.

"Mom and Dad had several dogs while I was growing up. I even rescued a beagle puppy on a highway one time."

"On a highway?"

"I was sixteen, or maybe seventeen at the time. As I was driving to school one morning, there was a little beagle puppy on the highway. I jumped out of my truck in rush hour traffic and rescued it."

"Oh, God. I would have been scared to death of getting killed."

"At that age you never worry about things like that. Guys don't, anyway."

"What about now?"

"What? Worry?"

"No, I meant once you were grown. Didn't you have a dog?"

"I traveled a lot. I wanted one but . . ." Ryan trailed off and stared out at the ocean.

Sara watched him as he gathered his thoughts.

"Well, my wife, or I should say *ex*-wife and I never had a dog."

Sara glanced down at his left hand. Sure enough, there was no wedding band on his ring finger, nor was there a telltale tan line. "How long were you married, if you don't mind my asking?"

"Eight years. Her name was Ann."

"Any children?"

"No. No kids or dogs. Did you and your ex have any children?" Ryan asked, looking over at her.

Sara did not speak at first; she was taken aback by Ryan's question. She knew she hadn't mentioned that she was divorced.

"I'm sorry. I just assumed you weren't married. I mean, there was no ring, and each time we met, it was just you and Molly here at the beach."

"My, you certainly are an observant one, aren't you?" Sara flashed a quick smile at Ryan. It felt good to be having a conversation with a man. Other than work and related topics at school, she really did not have anyone to just talk to. Not like this.

"My divorce . . ." Sara started to say, before she hesitated. "I mean, *our* divorce . . ." Sara stopped herself again, mid-sentence, and she tried to find the right words. Finally she said, "It took two of us to create a relationship, and I assume it's only fair that he share in the divorce as well. Right?"

Ryan said nothing in reply. He only listened, allowing Sara to express what she was feeling.

"Our divorce has been final for eight months now. We had one beagle and no children. Another divorce statistic, I assume." She stopped there, realizing she'd said more than enough.

As Ryan walked beside Sara, he wondered to himself why on earth any man would have ever let her go.

"And you?" Sara asked.

"I've been divorced for eighteen months."

Sara noticed the muscles in Ryan's jaw tighten as he answered her question. They strolled along the beach in silence for the next few moments, watching Molly as she sniffed and inspected everything she encountered in her path. It was as if the beach was filled with hidden treasures that were waiting to be discovered by her.

"I take it the divorce was not what you wanted," Ryan said at last, picking up where they had left off as he looked over at Sara.

"I had no idea he was so unhappy," Sara said, while she stared out at the ocean. "I guess I should have." She turned her attention back to Ryan and added, "By the time I figured it out, he had already started another life with a younger woman."

The two made their way up and over a sand dune in silence as Molly ran back toward them. Ryan quickly bent down and gave Molly a scratch behind the ears as they continued their walk.

"And you . . . is it what you wanted?" Sara asked.

"It was really my fault. I traveled far too much. The amount of time I spent away from her and from home was a blueprint for divorce. I just figured that out far too late to make a difference."

"What? You traveled a lot as a cattle rancher?"

Ryan looked over at Sara. "Cattle rancher? Oh, you're referring to the boots again." He smiled at her and gave his trademark wink. "She fell out of love with me. Can you imagine that?" Ryan said jokingly.

They both had a good laugh at Ryan's response, but then Sara wondered deep down inside if his joking was just a façade he used to mask his pain. They had been discussing their lives with smiles and laughter and relative ease as they walked in companionable silence, eventually coming full circle until they stood in the exact same spot they had stood at earlier that morning.

Ryan took that very moment to ask, "Do you know any good restaurants around here?"

Sara didn't even have to think about her response. "The Shoreline Inn is nice."

"Would you care to join me tonight?" Suddenly Ryan was surprised at himself for having asked.

Sara thought about it for a moment, then said, "I

can't, really . . . I have Molly with me."

"So you and Molly don't eat while you're here?"

Sara felt nervous and a little uncomfortable. This was the first time a man had asked her out since her divorce. All she could manage in response was: "The Inn we're staying at used to belong to my grandparents before they passed away. It's a long story, but the buyers had some issues with their banker. I ended up taking payments directly from them. Since the divorce, the income from the sale has really helped."

"That still doesn't explain why you and Molly don't eat while you're here."

Sara acted as though she didn't hear a word he said. "It was an agreement we made before the sale. I took payments from them, which helped them out, and since they knew how I felt about the place, they agreed to let Molly and me stay here anytime we felt the need to get away.

"You eat with the new owners?" Ryan asked, attempting to mask his frustration when she did not respond with a direct answer.

"When the new owners turned it into a bed and breakfast, they added a room downstairs. That's the room I always stay in. I actually have a grill sitting right outside my room in the back. "I can't leave Molly alone . . . at the . . . inn." Sara hesitated after taking note of Ryan's dejected expression. She realized that she had let him down by refusing his invitation to dinner.

Ryan crossed his arms over his chest and said nothing.

Moved by Ryan's disappointment, Sara blurted, "You could join Molly and me tonight for dinner instead. I had plans to grill up some scrod."

She had heard herself say it, but she could not believe she had actually uttered the words. What in the world could she have been thinking? She had just invited Ryan to have dinner with her and Molly. Her mind suddenly whirled with a strange mixture of emotions.

Ryan suddenly snapped back to himself, and the thought of a home-cooked meal drew a hasty response from him. "What can I bring?" Just the idea of having dinner with Sara was enough to bring a big smile to his face.

"Why don't you bring the wine?" Sara said, smiling back at him.

Chapter Eight

SARA'S MIND WAS STILL in a cloud as she rushed back to the inn. Her cell phone rang just as she opened the door to her room. It was Jane, her best friend. Jane was an attorney who worked for one of Boston's oldest and most prestigious law firms. Despite that, her friends and colleagues still considered her a little eccentric. Before Sara and Russ' breakup, Russ would tease Jane whenever she would visit their home in Norwood; in fact, he took great pleasure in it. Oftentimes, he would ask her if batteries were included with her outfit.

Needless to say, Jane never let anyone's comments affect her or change the way she dressed or acted. She handled her day-to-day life in her own unique way. Jane was what many women called "a golfer's widow," not that Jake—her husband of twenty-five years—was dead. Rather, Jake, busy as he was being a doctor, so loved his game of golf that every weekend he would leave Jane alone with their little two-year-old West Highland White Terrier, Max. For Jane, Max was much like a child who filled the empty nest after their two children, Jack and Gail, had grown up and started lives of their own. Poor Max was never allowed to be just a dog. He had a complete wardrobe along with matching booties, and Jane dressed him up everyday without fail. Whenever Jane brought Max to visit Molly and Sara, Molly would sniff Max's outfit while looking up at Jane and Sara as though she was asking what was wrong with him. Nevertheless, Sara figured that their visits were the only time Max could break free of Jane's constant fussing and doting over him. In fact, every time Max came over his clothes would usually be found in a pile in Sara's backyard as the little Westie ran around and rolled in the grass with Molly to his heart's content. Sara also knew that as soon as Jane got home, Max would be in the bathtub, where all traces of the day's play, which marked him as a real dog, would be removed. That said, it was nice for Max to be a dog at least some of the time.

"Hi, dear," Jane said—even on the phone her motherly tone was apparent. "I know you need time to get your thoughts together, but you know me . . . I just had to call and check on you."

Sara smiled as she tried to picture Jane perched in her cream colored chaise with Max dressed up in his latest outfit as he slept on her lap.

"I'm doing fine."

"You sound a little nervous, dear."

Sara took a breath, and before she could put her thoughts into words, Jane fired off a question.

"Is everything okay there? I knew I should have taken a break from the Peterson case and gone with you."

Sara thought about Ryan and their imminent dinner together, which was a few hours away. Try as she might, she was unable to hide the mixture of excitement and stress in her voice.

"Well . . . there's this man, ah–" Before Sara could finish her sentence, Jane interrupted.

"A man! You met a man! What is he like? Is he good looking? Tell me more!"

Sara knew from all their years of friendship that, by now, Jane had set little Max down so as to not wake him up and was probably on the edge of her seat.

"He's staying here at the inn," Sara said, offering no more, and almost enjoying the suspense she was building up.

"And?" Impatient for more details Jane repeated herself. "And?"

"He's different . . . in a, well, ah . . . refreshing way."

"Different . . . refreshing . . . that can be good, I suppose. But different how?" Jane asked, in a concerned tone.

"I really can't explain."

Sara cradled the phone between her ear and shoulder as she reached down to unhook Molly from her leash. After closing the door to the room, she sat down on the bed and felt herself smiling as she thought about Ryan and their walk on the beach.

"Oh dear God, he isn't married, is he?"

Sara chuckled at Jane's assumption. "No he isn't married. He's been divorced for eighteen months now."

Just as she spoke, Sara looked down at her wristwatch and remembered the dinner she had promised Ryan. She still had to run to the market before she could begin the meal's preparation.

"Jane, listen, I have to go get some fish for tonight. I invited Ryan to dinner this evening."

"Ryan—dinner—tonight—wait, he's coming to dinner?"

"Jane, I'll call you tomorrow and fill you in. Gotta go. Love ya. Bye."

Sara quickly ended the call before Jane could get another word in. She started for the door and grabbed her purse in the process. Seeing the keys in Sara's hand, Molly wagged her tail in excitement.

"Come on, Molly. But you'll have to stay in the car," Sara said, pointing.

Molly needed no direction and quickly scampered toward the car, stopping only when she reached the passenger side door. The beagle ran around in circles before jumping into the front seat. She loved to go for a ride, no matter how short or long the distance.

At the general store, Sara carefully inspected the fresh fish through the glass display before selecting two pieces of scrod. She quickly picked up two potatoes, a bag of salad fixings, and a locally made lemon meringue pie for dessert, putting each item in the cart with haste.

Karen, who had worked at the general store for years, rang up the items. Sara impatiently looked at her watch as Karen slowly bagged the items and counted out her change.

When she finally got back to her room she put the groceries in the small refrigerator and took a quick shower.

Next, she carefully sorted through the clothes she had brought with her. She wished she had packed nicer things. Then again, she hadn't expected to be inviting a man she barely knew to have dinner with her. After careful deliberation, she chose a bright yellow scoop neck blouse and a pair of canary yellow slacks to match. She took more time than usual with her hair and makeup, naturally, and after one last look in the mirror, she swiveled from side to side, hands on her hips, as she checked her reflection. What stared back at her got a short nod of approval. As a final touch, she reached for a bottle of Eternity and dabbed a bit of it on the nape of her neck and behind her ears. Although expensive, perfume was one of the few personal items that Sara splurged on.

"What d'ya think, Molly girl?"

Molly barked in response.

Now that she was dressed, she fed Molly her dinner and went out into the backyard to light the grill. No sooner had she lifted the cover than something prompted her to look around. The old house had a million wonderful childhood memories for her. She had often stayed with her grandparents during the summer months. The swing her grandfather had constructed in his woodworking shop still hung from the old maple tree, and her grandmother's garden mums still surrounded the white gazebo at the edge of the property line. Sara was thankful that she had been able to maintain a good friendship with the new owners over the years; this was part of the reason she and Molly were allowed to stay at the old house whenever they wanted.

Having turned her attention back to the grill, she lit it and watched the burners ignite just as a knock came at the door. Molly barked and ran toward the sound, wagging her tail. Sara found her sniffing the bottom of the door when she went to open it. Ryan stood on the other side of the door with a small Styrofoam cooler in hand, which Sara regarded with a confused expression as she invited him into her room.

Ryan offered a quick explanation: "I picked up a bottle of wine. I wanted it to stay chilled so I purchased a cooler and some ice."

Sara laughed as she took the cooler and set it down. Ryan caught the sweet scent of her perfume. He watched her as she crossed the room and he noticed how beautiful she looked.

"Would you like to sit out back while I get dinner going?" Sara asked, opening the sliding glass door that led to the backyard.

"Sure." Ryan followed her. "Wow, what a view you have from this room," he said, his eyes darting everywhere.

Sara motioned toward two white Adirondack chairs that sat next to the side of the old bed and breakfast. "Please, make yourself comfortable."

"Do you need me to do anything?" Ryan asked, refusing to take a seat.

"Would you open the wine for me? I have a basket inside with dishes and utensils in it. There's a wine opener in the flap on the inside lid."

"You bet."

Sara smiled. Ryan stood for a moment and

looked at her face. The few times they had met on the beach he was sure she had been crying. He was glad he could make her smile.

Ryan went back inside and found the opener and two wine glasses. He poured them each a glass and brought them outside, and then he carefully set them on the table between the two chairs. That done, he asked, "Anything else I can do?"

"You can keep Molly company. She's quite a food hound when I'm fixing dinner and is always underfoot."

"Is that true, Molly?" Ryan sat down and began to play with her.

Sara watched the two of them interacting with each other. Just seeing the two of them together as she fixed dinner made her feel comfortable. She wasn't really sure why, but for the first time in her life she didn't try to second-guess her feelings.

Noticing the temperature on the grill, she turned and went inside. She washed the potatoes and lightly applied butter to them before wrapping them in foil. Upon returning to the grill, she saw Ryan and Molly sitting down by the old gazebo. She set the potatoes on the grill and walked down to meet them.

"Beautiful, isn't it?" she said, sitting down next to Ryan.

"I've always wanted to build one." Ryan stood

and rubbed his hand along the railing, admiring the fine craftsmanship and the great attention to detail.

"My grandfather built this for my grandmother on their 30th wedding anniversary. She loved to sit out here for hours and read, and listen to the ocean."

"I can see why," Ryan said, as he sat back down. "It's beautiful."

"I just put the potatoes on. They'll need a head start."

"I brought your glass of wine." Ryan pointed toward it. "I hope it's okay, I told the guy at the liquor store that you were fixing scrod."

Sara sat down and took a sip. "Mmm, has a great taste. What is it?"

"Pinot Grigio."

Chapter Nine

AFTER DINNER, SARA AND Ryan cleaned up their dishes and retreated to the gazebo with two more glasses of wine, where they sat with Molly lying between them.

They sipped their drinks as Sara shared stories about the summers she had spent with her grandparents. When the glasses were empty, Ryan suggested: "Why don't we walk off our dinner on the beach?"

"Let me run in and get our jackets," Sara said, as she picked up the wine glasses.

Soon they were walking along the shoreline, neither of them noticing the chill in the air, now that the sun had set. The ocean was a vast shiny black pool of liquid as the light from the harvest moon danced across the waves.

Ryan caught a glimpse of how pretty Sara's dark eyes were as they sparkled in the moonlight. With only the light of the moon she was stunning. He wanted to tell her how beautiful she looked, but instead he said, "Dinner was delicious. I've never had scrod before. I really liked it." He bent down and picked up a small rock.

"I'm glad," Sara said, smiling.

"Not that it's any of my business, but the inn is such a beautiful old house. Why didn't you and your husband move into it instead of selling it?"

Sara thought about Ryan's question. It was a question that had pained her for years. She had long agonized over her decision, even before the ink had dried on the real estate contract she had signed in that large conference room in her attorney's office many years ago. Just the thought of that day was enough to bring tears to her eyes.

She held the tears back now as she offered the answer to Ryan's question: "I wanted to. While I could have changed school districts, it was too far for Russ to commute to work each day."

"He couldn't have gotten a job here?"

Sara smiled at the innocence in Ryan's question and shook her head at the thought. "No," she said, simply. "Russ works as a financial planner for a very prestigious firm in downtown Boston. Brant Rock, on the other hand, is not exactly a Mecca for their type of clientele."

"It does seem untarnished and untouched by the big city life, I'll give you that," Ryan said, as he looked out over the ocean. Then he posed another question: "So, what was Russ like?"

Sara hesitated for a moment, and looked down

as she thought about Russ. "He was tall and very handsome," she said finally. "Aggressive when it came to business and climbing the ladder of success. . . ."

Ryan listened to her in silence, not wanting to interrupt.

". . . Maybe too aggressive," Sara said, continuing her assessment of Russ.

"What do you mean by that?"

Sara turned and looked out over the ocean as though she was searching for an answer. The fact was, in all the months that followed the divorce; she still did not fully understand Russ' reason for the affair.

"The other woman . . ." she began to say, ". . . she was the sister of a senior partner at Russ' firm. Shortly after the affair started, Russ moved up the corporate ladder at a rapid pace, unbeknownst to me at the time."

Ryan noticed Sara dabbing a tear as it began to roll down her cheek. In what seemed like one swift movement, he reached out both arms, wrapped them around Sara, and held her close. Sara felt the warmth of Ryan's body against hers and there was no impulse to pull away. While they embraced, with the moon aglow above them, she felt the pain slip away.

In as soft a voice as he could manage, Ryan said

in her ear: “I’m sorry. I guess I shouldn’t have asked,” and then he slowly let go of her.

“No, it’s okay,” Sara said as they began to walk again. “I’ve needed to talk about this for months and just couldn’t.”

Ryan walked beside her in silence again, listening as she talked.

“He said it started out as just sex at first . . .” Sara said, hesitating a little. “Like that was supposed to make me feel better.”

Sara looked over at Ryan, shaking her head with a look of confusion on her face.

Ryan paused for a moment before speaking. “I really don’t know what to say to that.” But he chose his next words carefully. “I guess I’ve never understood the mechanics of an affair. I believe that if someone is unhappy and wants out of a relationship, they should just leave and allow the other person to keep their dignity.”

Ryan reached over and took Sara’s hand as they continued to walk. The action had been as natural as that of two people who had known each other for years. Her hand felt soft in his, and right.

Ryan continued his thought: “I think people who have affairs want a safety net.”

“A safety net?” Sara questioned.

“Yeah. Like if this doesn’t work out with the new person, I still have the other person as a safety net I can go back to," Ryan said, expanding on his theory.

Sara thought about Ryan's view. She had often wondered how long Russ would have carried on the affair before being man enough to tell her the truth. It made sense that she was Russ' safety net. She was sure that if she hadn't found out, Russ wouldn't have ended the affair. The thought of this was not appealing in the least. However, Ryan's theory, right or wrong, did not hurt her. Rather, it made her mad to think that Russ may have stayed with her only to have someone to fall back on in case the other relationship did not work out as planned.

Nevertheless, she could not allow the anger she felt toward Russ to ruin their evening, which would further allow Russ control over her emotions. So she let it go. When she tossed her wedding band into the ocean earlier that day, she vowed to move forward with her life. With that in mind, Sara quickly changed the subject.

"So," she said, running a hand through her hair, "what is it you really do when you aren't visiting little New England towns and playing with beagles you happen to meet on the beach?"

Ryan thought about his work and his fear that it was the one thing that had driven him and Ann apart. He struggled with his words. "I write." He felt his throat tighten with the answer. He studied Sara's face in the moonlight, gauging her reaction.

All she said was, "Books?"

"No. I'm a journalist. Although I *have* thought about writing a book for years, I just never got around to it. Cattle ranching in New Mexico had been my life before that, but my dad's passing changed everything, and my heart just wasn't in it anymore. I landed a few writing assignments as a freelance journalist for a local newspaper, then *The Post* took me on fulltime."

"Are you here in Brant Rock writing an article about the town?" she asked, with excitement in her voice.

Ryan felt something stir within him as he held Sara's hand; they were feelings he had not allowed himself to feel for a long time. He wondered if Sara felt the same way.

"No," he said. "I'm here for two weeks of R and R. I spend six weeks on an assignment and two weeks off."

"This is so interesting. I bet my students would love to hear about your work."

Ryan's jaw clenched just as he was about to speak. "Sara, no. You don't understand."

Sara stopped short, her own expression a mask of confusion. "What is it that I don't understand?"

Ryan's face was rigid now. "The type of journalism I do . . . it's not something that the kids need to hear about."

Ryan let go of her hand as they continued to walk. He felt himself closing off.

Sara pressed him for an answer. "Okay, then what type of journalism do you do?"

He did not answer at first. While he knew she had a perfect right to ask, he still feared telling her. Reluctantly, he told Sara in a quiet voice, "I'm an embedded journalist with troops at this time."

Sara had heard accounts on the evening news about journalists being embedded with the US troops. She had also heard about journalists as well as their crews being killed in war torn countries. She was suddenly fearful of Ryan's safety. He would be here in the states for a mere two weeks, she thought to herself; two weeks and then what?—and what's worse, then *where*? Would she ever see him again? Like everyone else, Sara wondered if the war would ever end.

Finally she asked him, "What type of stories did they have you covering before the war?" She knew she was searching here, but she wanted to hear something good about his career as a journalist; something that didn't involve war.

"I've been sent all over the world to cover global events like the civil unrest in Bosnia, Africa,

Afghanistan, the Gaza Strip, and many other countries."

Sara felt a knot form in the pit of her stomach. While she attempted to absorb not only this new information about what he did for a living, she also felt herself struggling with the feelings she was having for Ryan. While they had just met, deep down in her soul, she felt that she had known him all of her life.

"Penny for your thoughts," Ryan said, as he rubbed the smooth rock he'd picked up between his thumb and first two fingers. It was an old tradition many Indians in New Mexico still practice to this day to relieve stress.

Sara snapped out of her contemplative state and said, "I was wondering if we'll ever see each other again—after tonight I mean."

The thought had crossed Ryan's mind as well. There was just something about Sara that had attracted him from the moment he first saw her, though he couldn't quite put his finger on it.

"I guess that would depend on us . . ." he said, turning in mid-sentence to toss the small rock into the dark ocean, ". . . and whether or not we wanted to see each other again." Ryan turned to her and added, "I know I'd like to see you again."

Sara suddenly felt like a teenager. She had hated dating as a teenager, and she'd even hated it when she attended college, but for some reason this was different. Ryan was different.

"I would like that," she said, almost blushing as she took Ryan's hand in hers and looked into his hazel eyes.

"The water looks so different at night," Ryan said, as he turned to face the ocean.

"My grandfather always said it looked like a pool of oil at night—because of the reflection from the dark sky above, I suppose."

Sara looked out across the water. Ryan noticed her shiver from the night's chill, so he moved in close behind her, wrapped his arms around her midsection, and held her tightly as they stood in silence, looking out over the sea. Sara could feel the warmth and strength of his body, and she had a sudden overwhelming desire to turn around and kiss him at that very moment. Reminding herself that they had met only a few days ago, she fought off the urge. Being with Ryan seemed almost surreal.

Ryan suddenly let go of Sara and placed his hands on her shoulders, gently turning her until she faced him. He gazed deep into those dark brown eyes of hers and noticed, again, how beautiful they were in the moonlight. Without uttering a word, and scarcely breathing, he moved in closer to her, leaned in slightly, and kissed her softly on the lips. His hand gently caressed her shoulders and then moved slowly down her back. Sara leaned in as well, while the warmth and passion of his kiss made her weak in the knees and left her feeling a little lightheaded. Sara felt the passionate sensation wash over her completely. Ryan stopped and looked deep into her eyes again, and again he kissed her. After several more kisses, Sara finally pulled away.

"We better head back to the inn," she told him. "I have to get up early and pack. I'm going back home in the morning."

With that, they walked in silence back to the bed and breakfast.

As they stepped into her room, Ryan found himself not wanting to say goodbye. When he got ready to leave, he turned back toward Sara. Acting on a strong impulse, he pulled her close and kissed her passionately once more.

He gave her a pleading look. "I don't want this to end. Can't you stay a bit longer? I'll be here for two weeks."

"Ryan, I have to get back. The new school year will be starting next week."

Ryan kissed her again, and this time he placed tiny kisses along the neckline of her blouse as well. He stopped only to gaze longingly into her dark eyes before he resumed kissing her again. Sara pulled away and locked the door. Taking Ryan by the hand, she led him over to the bed, lit two candles, and turned on the radio. She walked back over to him and began to unbutton his shirt. His chest was tanned and muscular. There was something so right about tonight; so right about *him* that it outweighed any logic in her mind. She had never been this bold, not even when she had dated Russ. The anticipation of his touch, and the sensation of actually feeling it, warm and gentle against her skin, was an irresistible combination that sent chills down her spine. Ryan slowly unbuttoned her blouse and marveled at how beautiful she looked in that moment. They stood naked before each other for a few seconds before embracing in the candlelight. Then Sara made her way over to the bed and laid down on it, reaching her hand out to Ryan. He took her hand in his and gently kissed each finger, before he ran kisses along her arm—and during all this he never took his eyes away from hers. He applied a series of kisses to her other hand and arm, and as he continued to kiss her he moved to her breasts. Ryan's movements were careful and deliberate, and he was extremely gentle with her, yet they made love with a sense of urgency, releasing their growing desires for each other with abandon. They made love three times, slowly and tenderly exploring each other's bodies as they did so. When it was over, Ryan lay awake in the moonlight and watched Sara drift off to sleep. While wrapped in each other's arms, he got to thinking, and he somehow figured that if the mistakes of the past had brought them together then maybe this time they had both finally got it right. Eventually, the sound of her rhythmic breathing lulled him to sleep.

❧

RYAN WAS ROUSED SOMEWHAT by a warm, moist tongue that licked his arm. Half asleep, he smiled and mumbled Sara's name. As he turned over and reached out for her, Molly gave him another lick on his arm. This one, however, was accompanied by a shove with her cold, wet nose. Startled, Ryan sat up in bed.

"What do you think of my beagle alarm clock?" asked Sara, as she walked in holding a dishtowel.

Ryan sat down on the edge of the bed, rubbing the sleep from his eyes. "Beagle kisses . . . you know, a guy could get used to this!" he joked.

"Breakfast is almost ready if you want to get cleaned up. I put a clean towel in the bathroom for you."

Ryan took a hot shower and toweled off. He ran his fingers through his hair, combing it back from his forehead as he made a mental note to drop by a barbershop before his next assignment. After he got dressed, he slowly walked into the front room. The delectable aroma of freshly cooked bacon and eggs filled the air. Sara had her back to him as she stood over the apartment-sized stove. He walked over, wrapped his arms around her, and kissed the back of her neck. Sara closed her eyes, savoring both his touch and embrace.

The moment was interrupted just then as Molly scratched the side door wanting out.

"Molly, you have such great timing," Sara said, shaking her head.

"I'll take her outside." Ryan grabbed his jacket and headed for the door, which got Molly to wag her tail.

Sara turned and watched the two of them. Molly's tail never stopped wagging as she ran around and played out back with Ryan. Everything seemed perfect—everything except that in two weeks Ryan would be half a world away, that is. Despite this, and the fact that she had to leave for home today, she knew she wanted to spend more time with him. After shaking the feeling off the best she could, she called Ryan and Molly back inside.

Moments later, while looking at Ryan over her cup of coffee, Sara said, "I want you to know that I've never done this before—what happened last night."

"Any regrets?" Ryan asked, with a concerned look on his face.

"No. Not at all." She stood up, walked over to him, and sat in his lap.

"I don't have any myself," Ryan said, as he held her, "but I guess what's most important is what you want from this point forward."

Sara ran her fingers through his hair, messing it up. "I know you have reservations here for two weeks, but why don't you come home with Molly and me? I'll have to work during the day but we could spend the evenings together."

Sara hoped he would say yes. This would give both of them more time to explore this new relationship. She studied Ryan's face, attempting to read his expression, but she couldn't.

He made it easy for her, however, saying, "I'd like that," and then he smiled, and kissed her.

Chapter Ten

ON THE DRIVE BACK TO Norwood, Ryan followed Sara and Molly in his rental car. Sara smiled as she looked in the rearview mirror. She felt almost giddy inside as she watched Ryan driving behind her. Just the thought of last night, being wrapped in his arms, made her tingle all over. *God,* she thought, *it's been a long time since I've felt this way. Too long.*

Suddenly she remembered that she hadn't called Jane. She reached over and grabbed the headset for her cell phone and pressed a speed dial key on the phone itself.

Sara turned off the interstate while she waited for Jane to answer her call. After two rings she heard Jane's voice. "Hello."

"Hey, how is your Sunday going?" Sara inquired.

"Hey yourself, young lady. Where have you been? I haven't heard from you. You had me worried sick."

"Mom?" Sara said jokingly, and laughed. "Jane, really, Ryan is a very nice man."

"Sweetie they're all nice—at first. You've just got

to find one that will stick around—like my Jakie."

"He is . . . well at least I think he's that type."

After Jane's interrogation, Sara finally knew what people on the witness stand must feel like when being questioned by this high-priced Boston attorney. However, there was one detail Sara had omitted: that Ryan was going to spend the rest of his time in New England—at her house.

BACK AT SARA'S HOUSE, Molly ran around as though she was giving Ryan the grand tour of her backyard. Sara stood at the back window and watched him playing with Molly for a few minutes. Then she began unpacking her things and sorting her dirty clothes into piles, and she wondered when she would find the time to get all of the laundry done. Next, she put a clean set of sheets on her bed. As she tossed the dirty sheets into the laundry basket, intending to take them downstairs to the washer, she noticed the divorce papers on her dresser. She quickly opened the top drawer and tossed the papers inside. That done, she then hung fresh towels in the bathroom, including a second set alongside hers for Ryan. She glanced over at the second set hanging next to hers and smiled. When Russ had moved out, it was the simple things, like her single towel, that constantly reminded her of the void the divorce had left.

She had been down in the basement starting the sheets on the wash cycle when she heard Ryan and Molly coming back inside.

"Do you have any clothes that need to be washed?" she shouted, over the hum of the washing machine. "I'll have another load going in soon."

"You sure you don't mind?" Ryan called out from upstairs.

"No, not at all."

Ryan gathered up a few things from his duffle bag and brought them down to her. As he stood behind her, he wrapped his arms around her, and kissed her on the back of the neck.

"I was just wondering," he said, "since you're back home, and Molly is in her own house, could I possibly take you out to dinner tonight?"

Sara's mind ran through a long list of things she had to get done before returning to work in the morning.

Noticing the troubled look on her face, Ryan asked, "What is it?"

"It's just that I have three more loads of laundry to do and—"

Ryan interrupted her. "If you sort them out, I can do them in the morning while you're at work."

Sara could not believe what she was hearing. She was certain she must have heard wrong.

"Really, I don't mind," Ryan assured her. "I'll be here while you're at work. As long as you sort them out, I can do them up. This way we can spend more time together."

"Okay," Sara said, trying not to sound shocked by his offer. Russ would never have done laundry, even if he took a few days off and she was at work. Russ was always too busy watching sports on television or golfing with buddies.

"Why don't you make the reservations for tonight. Wherever you want to go."

Sara picked one of her favorite Italian restaurants, Landini's, just off Route 1. It overlooked a golf course, but Sara loved their food and the ambiance created by the soft candlelight. She had not been there since she and Russ had split up. She told herself that she could not afford such luxuries, but the truth was she hated dining alone. She knew she shouldn't feel that way. After all, a woman eating out alone was mysterious, she told herself many times. Nevertheless, that would only last until she picked up her purse and walked toward the front door. Each time she tried to leave, however, she would end up turning back, setting her purse down, and staying in with Molly.

Ryan seemed to like her choice. As they entered the restaurant he looked around and gave an accepting nod. They waited only a few moments before the hostess found a quiet table for two in a cozy corner of the restaurant. Ryan pulled her chair out for her and helped her off with her coat as she took a seat.

To their right, a large stone fireplace warmed the room. The flames seemed to dance to the soft sound of Pachelbel's *Canon* playing in the background. Sara ordered her favorite dish, Five-cheese Ziti. Ryan ordered Eggplant Parmesan and a bottle of the house wine. When the wine arrived, Ryan looked into her eyes and lifted his glass.

"To the most beautiful woman I know."

Sara felt herself blush crimson as Ryan made his toast.

Ryan teased her, saying, "You look good in red," as he gave a soft chuckle.

Sara had to admit—if only to herself—how much she loved his quick wit and the way he made her feel when he opened doors for her or pulled her chair out.

"Central New Mexico, what is it like out west?" Sara asked, as she reached across the table and ran her finger over Ryan's hand.

"Different. Long stretches of bare land as far as the eye can see. Beautiful, majestic mountains and some of the most beautiful sunsets that most people only see in coffee table books. Nevertheless, it is a desert and can be extremely dry.

Ryan paused when the waiter brought them their salads.

"Sounds spectacular," Sara said, just before she took a bite of a vine-ripened tomato.

"Have you ever traveled west of New England?"

"Never. I'm strictly a northeastern girl, I'm afraid." Sara took a sip of her wine.

"Nothing wrong with that, but we should go out West just so you can see how pretty it is."

"We'd fly out there?"

"Actually, Ma'am, we do have an airport," Ryan said, in his best southern drawl. "We gave up on the stagecoach years ago."

"Wise guy, huh?" Sara said, playfully nudging his leg with her foot under the table. "You'll have to take me there someday."

"Sure, why not? We could go next month. Each year in October, Albuquerque hosts the International Balloon Fiesta." Ryan stopped and looked at Sarah. "We could go out there and I could show you around."

Sara had seen photos of the event last year on the news. She even had her class do a report on the various hot air balloons that flew that year. "I'll see if I can get a few days off," Sarah said, mentally calculating how many personal days she had left.

The waiter quietly placed their dinner before

them without interrupting their conversation.

"Then it's a deal. I'll make the arrangements for a trip to Albuquerque following my next assignment."

Now that they were on the subject of work, Sara dabbed her napkin against her lips and told him, "I would like to know more about your work and what it's like being an embedded journalist."

"Well, let's see. What can I tell you? Lip balm is a commodity. Your lips get so dry, chapped, and cracked. I think I could make enough money to retire if I was a lip balm salesman over there."

Sara laughed. Ryan could see she wanted to know more.

"Do you know what MREs are?"

Sara furrowed her brows in thought. "It sounds like an acronym for something . . . I guess."

"You're right. They are packaged meals the military calls Made Ready to Eat, but we call them Meals Rejected by the Enemy."

Sara burst into laughter.

Ryan kept it going, saying, "Me and my buddy, Al, always take some red chili sauce with us. No matter what the MRE is, I can doctor it up and give it some flavor with a little chili sauce."

"You make this sound like a segment on The Cooking Channel." Sara smiled at him.

Ryan watched her reaction and began to think

that maybe his work wouldn't be an issue with Sara after all.

She continued. "So, we need to pack you some chili sauce and lip balm before you go. Anything else?"

"Bandannas and baby wipes."

Sara raised her eyebrows in confusion as she echoed his words: "Bandannas and baby wipes."

"The bandannas are to put over your nose and mouth. I even use one when I sleep." He could tell Sara still did not understand. "They keep the sand from getting into your nose and mouth."

"Oh, I see," Sara said, nodding. "And the baby wipes?"

"Baby wipes are as important as lip balm. You can use them to clean yourself and your equipment when out on an assignment."

Sara found herself making mental notes with regard to the various items Ryan would need before he left, and all of this based on what he was telling her now. She began to ask, "But, what about . . . ?" but she couldn't finish her sentence. She fidgeted with the edge of her napkin, folding and refolding it.

Ryan knew that Sara wanted and needed to know more about his assignments than lip balm and baby wipes. With that in mind, he said, "Look, I know what you've probably heard on the local and national news. I'm not going to try to convince you that it's a day in the park. It isn't. It's war."

Ryan hesitated, gathering his thoughts. Then he added, "The one thing I can tell you is that the military makes every effort to keep the journalists safe."

"But what about . . . ?"

Ryan took both of Sara's hands in his. There was no way to sugarcoat what he did for a living. The bottom line was that he worked in a war zone.

"I know where you're going with this, honestly I do, and I understand," Ryan said softly, as he sat forward and turned to look at her in silence. He wondered if his line of work, and the places it took him would be something that Sara could eventually get use to. Or would it drive them apart, like it did with Ann?

After dinner they ordered some coffee and talked some more, and as they did the subject would gravitate beyond Ryan's work but would somehow manage to work its way back to what he did for a living. Sara realized that no matter how long they talked, or despite the way Ryan described his work, the end result was still the same. She was not going to hear what she wanted to.

After dinner, they returned home and curled up in each other's arms on the couch with Molly at their feet.

The old oak grandfather clock chimed eleven times. Knowing that tomorrow would be her first day back at school, she stood up. She took Ryan's hand and led him upstairs and they prepared for bed. Ryan lay awake long after Sara drifted off to sleep. As he lay there listening to her soft breathing he stared at the ceiling. Deep in thought, he watched the shadowy patterns the tree limbs created as the breeze caused them to sway in front of the moon outside her bedroom window. Before he drifted off to sleep himself, he wondered if there was anything he could have said to her that could have changed her mind about what he did and where he worked.

SARA FOUND THAT SHE did not have her usual enthusiasm for the beginning of the school year. Each day she watched the clock, anticipating the very second she could go home to Ryan. Since he would be leaving soon, she decided to take a sick day mid-week and they drove to Maine for the day. They engaged in a leisurely stroll along streets that featured some old shops and they ate lunch at a quaint restaurant by the ocean. As Ryan looked out over the water, Sara admired the collection of teapots that lined the shelves above the tables.

The following day, the last school bell of the day

finally rang, and for the first time in a long time, she felt like one of the kids in class, anxious to leave the classroom at the end of the day. While clearing her desk, she noticed little Johnny Morris standing in front of her.

"Ms . . . ah, Ketcham . . . I lost my . . ." Johnny looked down at his shoes, then he slowly brought his eyes up again before finishing his statement: ". . . My English book."

Sara set her notepad down.

Little Johnny continued: "While you were gone, and . . . and we had Mr. Grumpy as our substitute teacher—"

"You mean Mr. Grundy, don't you?" Sara corrected.

"Yeah, Mr. Grumpy." Johnny was totally unaware that Sara had corrected him. "Anyway, that's why I didn't turn in my homework."

Sara could see how upset Johnny was. "Tell you what, in the morning I will go to the library and pick up a new one for you." She quickly wrote a note to herself referencing the book.

"But . . . my homework?"

"I will reassign it to you in the morning. How does that sound?"

"Cool! I mean, thank you, Ms. Ketcham," Johnny said, as he ran toward the door.

"No running in the classroom," Sara called out.

Johnny stopped and turned around. "Sorry Ms. Ketcham," he said, sheepishly, taking the last four steps toward the door at a snail's pace.

Sara watched him turn the doorknob. As soon as he was through the doorway, he burst into a full run. She shook her head and laughed to herself. She felt like doing the same thing. How would it look if she, a grown woman, and a teacher no less, left the classroom running? As she locked the classroom door, just the visual image of seeing herself breaking into a run made her smile. God knows, if old Mrs. Jefferson, the fourth grade teacher, had caught her doing it, the poor woman would have suffered a heart attack right on the spot.

When she finally got home, she noticed that Ryan had washed and folded the towels and had them sitting in a neat pile on her bed. She looked out the window at the backyard and found, much to her surprise, that Ryan had raked up the first of the fallen leaves from her three large maple trees and bagged them in preparation for trash day.

That night after dinner, they made love again until they drifted off to sleep in each other's arms. On Friday, Ryan found a set of tools in the old shed out back, which he used to fix a broken shutter on the north side of Sara's house. And later, on the same day, he took Molly for a walk before Sara got home. They were on their way back to the house when Mrs. Kelly spotted Ryan. It didn't matter that she recognized Molly. Sighting an unknown man in the neighborhood was enough to throw her radar into high gear.

Gladys Kelly was an elderly woman in her seventies. She was affectionately known to all in the neighborhood as "the resident nosey neighbor," and she was also known for her gumshoe instincts, which she used to gather each and every detail about everyone who lived on Sara's street.

That evening, Mrs. Kelly called Sara to get the complete rundown on who Ryan was exactly, how long he would be staying, and why he was there in the first place.

On Monday, Ryan busied himself by fixing the bathroom door while Sara was at school. Then he freshened up and made a trip to a barbershop he had spotted on Washington Street. Afterwards, he went home to pick up Molly, and they met Sara for lunch. They ate in the park not far from the school where Sara taught third grade. After he dropped her off at the school, Ryan began driving back to Sara's house when he saw a pet store. Fully aware that Molly was almost out of dog food, he stopped short.

Ryan took Molly into the store with him. Not only did he buy a bag of dog food, he also bought her a new squeaky toy she picked out and a brand new collar and matching leash.

Neither Sara nor Ryan talked about what would happen once his two-week stay in New England was up. Nonetheless, they both found themselves thinking about it. Sara found it harder and harder to hide her fears. She had to turn away to keep Ryan from seeing her tears well up and run down her cheeks when she thought about him leaving them and returning to work in some war torn country. As he put it he'd be gone six weeks and back home for two. She knew Ryan wanted her to go to New Mexico with him. What would happen after that, she pondered. *Would he want to come back to New England? Would he want to spend his time off with me?*

If someone would have told her a year ago, or even a month ago, that she could fall for a guy so quickly, she would have laughed in that person's face. To Sara, they seemed like the perfect couple. She was sure if she asked for Jane's input, which she hadn't, Jane would simply say that they were properly aligned with the universe and were on the same level. Jane not only had a colorful wardrobe but also a colorful way of looking at life. It was almost a whimsical detachment from her day-to-day life as a high-powered attorney.

Regardless, destiny, by way of a little coastal

New England town, had brought them together, when neither of them was looking for love.

Chapter Eleven

IN THE MORNING, SARA discovered that Jane had called and left a message on her cell phone; she and Jakie wanted to meet Ryan and her for dinner. Sara had still not told Jane that Ryan had been staying with her since she had returned to Norwood. She figured that Jane had probably put two and two together by now, as she hadn't been calling her every night like she usually did. Instead, Jane would call her during the day to check on her. Sara returned her calls on her break.

She put in a call to Jane just then and said, "Hey lady, know any good attorneys in Boston?" when Jane picked up.

"Just me!" Jane answered, and then got right down to business. "What do you think about dinner at The Tower tomorrow night? Jake and I would love to meet Ryan."

Sara smiled, knowing that poor Jake probably couldn't care less. Unless it involved eighteen holes and a set of golf clubs or watching the Red Sox play at Fenway Park, Jake was just along for the ride.

"Sure, I think that can be arranged," Sara said.

Jane asked, "Does that cowboy of yours eat seafood?"

"Loves it."

"Good boy! He is sounding better all the time. I'll be working late every evening on that darn Peterson case so why don't you both meet us at The Tower at 7:00 tomorrow evening?"

"Sounds like a plan. We'll meet you there."

That evening after dinner, Sara and Ryan did the dishes together. Sara explained that her best friend, Jane, and her husband, Jake, had invited them to one of the finest restaurants in Boston.

Standing in front of the kitchen sink, Ryan looked down at his denim jeans. "Hmmm, don't guess this is acceptable attire, is it?"

"Not really."

As soon as the dishes were done and put away, they went to the mall. Once there, Sara and Ryan headed straight for the clothing department, where the men's suits were located.

Ryan tried several jackets on; he fit perfectly into a size 44. He eventually found a taupe colored suit he liked two racks down from where Sara was looking at the dark blue ones. When Ryan turned to show her, he noticed Sara's expression change as a tall man approached her. Ryan was too far from them to hear the conversation.

Sara stood motionless, staring at Russ with a

befuddled expression."

"So, where did you find Cinderella?" Russ asked, pointing toward Ryan, who was wearing the taupe suit coat with his jeans and cowboy boots.

In all the months that Sara and Russ had been divorced, they had never once run into each other. Why on earth were they doing it now, she wondered.

"Oh, hello, Russ." Sara looked at her wristwatch. "Is it past Sandy's bedtime? Oh, of course it is. It's a school night."

Russ did not respond to Sara's cutting remark about his younger girlfriend. He knew Sara was deeply hurt by his affair with Sandy.

Ryan walked over to Sara's side.

Sara said, "Ryan, this is Russ, my *ex*-husband. Russ, this is Ryan Spencer."

"Stick to the blue or black—more businesslike," Russ said, as he winked at Ryan and pointed at the taupe jacket he was wearing.

"Nah, too stuffy, don't you think?" Ryan turned to Sara and modeled the jacket for her with confidence.

Sara held back laughter at Ryan's quick comeback. "Nice, very sexy. We need to find you a shirt and tie to match."

Sara put her arm around Ryan, turning him away from Russ. Then she looked back at Russ and said, "Excuse us, but we have to be going."

As Sara directed Ryan toward a display of men's dress shirts she turned and noticed Russ inspecting the taupe suits. Sara and Ryan found a suitable shirt and tie, and then completed the ensemble with a belt, socks, and shoes.

"There's just one thing," Ryan said, with his arms full of shopping bags as they left the store.

"What's that?"

"When I go back to work, can I leave all this with you?"

"Gee, Ryan, taupe is just not my color," Sara teased. "Of course you can leave it with me. Half of the bedroom closet is empty." Sara leaned over and kissed him.

The following day was unseasonably warm. Ryan wiped beads of sweat from his forehead with the back of his hand as he stood in front of the house. For the last hour he had busied himself by pruning a row of rose brushes that lined the driveway. After he cleaned up the trimmings that dotted the ground, he and Molly went inside to make some lunch.

At that moment, Russ slowly drove past the house he and Sara once shared. He noticed a rental car parked in the driveway. The yard looked immaculate. Even the shutter that Sara had asked him to fix months before they divorced was repaired. Russ found himself wondering who this guy was. He didn't look like he was from Massachusetts, nor did Russ remember him being a member of Sara's family. Russ felt his competitive nature kick in at the very moment he downshifted the BMW. He made the loop through the neighborhood and came back for a second pass by the house. Old Mrs. Kelly was at the curb pulling in her trashcan. Russ knew she would more than likely mention this to Sara. After pulling the Beamer over to the curb, he rolled down the passenger side window and said, "Hi, there."

"Hi yourself," Mrs. Kelly said. "Sara's not home."

"You know, I figured that."

"I just bet you did." Mrs. Kelly had not been fond of Russ since his affair. In fact, on a few occasions she had seen Russ and a young woman coming home at lunchtime in his fancy car, and she knew immediately that something was amiss.

"I have a ski trip planned in Vermont this weekend," Russ said. "Figured I would stop by and grab my skis out of our shed."

"*Our* shed? I thought you moved out months ago." Mrs. Kelly leaned down and peered into the passenger side window.

Russ instinctively pressed his elbow into the armrest as he tried to move as far away as he could from the wrinkled face that was staring at him.

"Why don't I just give Sara a call tonight and see if I can arrange to drop by sometime."

"Why don't you do that?" Mrs. Kelly commented sternly, before she moved away from the car and watched until Russ was out of sight.

Chapter Twelve

RYAN AND SARA ENTERED The Tower restaurant. Ryan immediately walked toward the windows that extended from floor to ceiling as Sara gave her name to the maitre d' and added, "Party of Jane Strause." Thirty-eight floors high atop one of Boston's tallest buildings, the view from the restaurant was breathtaking. Ryan peered out at Boston Harbor, mesmerized by the colorful vista. Boats, as well as the many nearby buildings with glass façades were casting shimmering rays of light onto the water, making it appear as though the water itself was illuminated. Ryan turned away from the window, and as he did, Sara flashed a quick smile at him.

"Hey cowboy. You clean up nice," she said.

Ryan straitened his tie and adjusted his jacket. "You think?"

Just then, a loud female voice called out, startling him. Ryan's first thoughts were that one of the restaurant's patrons had a little too much to drink during their meal. He turned and noticed a tall, slender woman with bright orange hair standing in the dining room entrance. She appeared to be in her early fifties. She wore a loud leopard print dress with matching heels and a purple silk scarf wrapped neatly around her neck. To Ryan's dismay, she was waving in their direction.

"Sweetie, over here!" Jane called out, motioning them toward her.

Ryan turned around in an attempt to see who this woman could be waving to.

Sara noticed the shocked look on his face, which made her feel like she had to offer an explanation: "She dresses a little differently."

"Really? I would never have noticed," Ryan said with a smile.

"You behave!"

After they made their way over to Jane, she grabbed Sara and gave her a big bear hug. "He's a looker. Love those dimples!" Jane whispered in her ear.

Jane turned her attention to Ryan next. She grabbed him and gave him a big hug as well, and Sara chuckled at the surprised look on his face.

"Oh, sweetie, I'm a hugger. You'll just have to get used to it," Jane said, as she moved away, looking Ryan over. "Mmm, mmm, mmm."

Ryan pulled on his collar and tie nervously and moved closer to Sara.

Jane added, "We reserved our favorite table.

Come on over. Jakie is waiting for us."

They all went into the dining room and took their seats. Their waiter, dressed in a black tux and tie, brought the menus over as if on cue and placed large cloth napkins on their laps. Jake ordered a bottle of Opus One Merlot and Kistler McCrea Chardonnay for the table.

"Unless you'd like something else?" Jake asked, looking at Ryan and Sara.

Neither objected.

Ryan glanced over the wine list in front of him, looking for anything he recognized.

"Jakie is quite the wine collector," Jane said, winking at Ryan and tapping his forearm with her finger.

Jake ignored his wife's antics and addressed Ryan: "Both are wonderful wines. I think you'll like them. Did you know the Opus One winery never reuses their French barrels?"

Ryan cleared his throat. "No I didn't." Before tonight he had never even heard of Opus One Merlot or Kistler McCrea. He worried now about his selection of wine for his and Sara's first dinner. *Was it nine dollars a bottle or fifteen*, he thought to himself as he looked at the wine prices on the menu? Sara noticed Ryan was well out of his comfort zone with all the wine talk.

"Jakie, how are your Red Sox doing this year?"

Sara inquired.

Jake quickly switched from talk of wine to a lively discourse on the Red Sox, and then he was on to his next love, golf. All the while Jane chatted away nonstop with Sara. Ryan glanced over the menu as he listened to Jake talk about his brand new pair of handcrafted golf shoes and the merits of having good equipment. Ryan took a sip of water and almost choked when Jakie mentioned the exorbitant cost of the shoes: $5,000 dollars.

"I don't play myself," Ryan said, "but I hope to learn someday." Anxious to change the subject, he then asked Jake, "What do you recommend for the main course?"

Jane stopped talking to Sara and gave her full attention to Ryan. "Sweetie, the lobster is out of this world," she said, "and their scrod. . . . Have you tried scrod yet?"

"Yes, actually. Sara made that for me when we were at Brant Rock."

"I always have the scrod stuffed with lobster when I eat here," Sara said.

"Scrod it is." Ryan said, closing his menu.

Ryan glanced around the restaurant while subconsciously tugging at his tie. He wasn't accustomed to wearing a suit and tie, other than to weddings and funerals. Once the entrees arrived he felt a sense of relief at no longer having to make small talk, with the exception of commenting on how good the food tasted.

After dinner, both Jane and Sara excused themselves to go to the ladies' room.

Jane leaned over the counter to reapply her lipstick and powder her nose while glancing at Sara's reflection behind her in the mirror. "Oh honey, he's a keeper!" Jane's loud voice echoed in the bathroom. "He's sweet. He has a charm about him, and doesn't seem like one of those guys who is so into themselves these days."

"Refreshing. I told you," Sara said, glancing at her own reflection in the mirror. "I think those are the qualities I first noticed about him and liked. But . . . there's more. . . ." Sara searched for the right words. "I feel like we've known each other forever. There's just something about him."

Jane thought for a moment. "You know how I feel about eternal love and fate."

"Oh, don't you start that again," Sara said, smiling at Jane in the mirror while she tossed all of her makeup back into the leopard print handbag.

Jane asked, "Will he be staying with you until he goes back to Iraq?"

Sara laughed. "Jane, does anything ever escape you?"

"Never. Just ask Jakie."

When Sara and Jane returned to the table Sara

smiled to herself after noticing that Ryan was nodding politely as he listened to Jake ramble on about some great new golf balls he had tried last weekend.

Jane insisted they all try a new dessert and she ordered for all of them. It turned out to be an elegant, but decadent Cold Zabaglione made with egg yolks, sugar, whipping cream, and sparkling Italian wine, and served with chocolate shavings on top.

After dessert, they said their goodbyes with handshakes and hugs and then they parted. On the commute back home, Sara told Ryan a little more about Jane, Jake, and Max, Jane's West Highland Terrier.

The following week, Ryan spent his days gathering up his supplies. He and Sara even went to a bookstore to pick up a few paperback books and magazines, which were to be given out to the troops—something Ryan had always done on his return trips.

The night before he was to leave, Ryan found Sara in tears more than once. He tried to reassure her that everything would be fine and that he would see her in six weeks, but he did so to no avail. The following morning when he woke up he reached over to Sara's side of the bed and found it empty. He got out of bed and went downstairs. Sara sat at the kitchen table with tear-stained cheeks. She was looking at Ryan's duffle bag, which sat on the floor by the backdoor. She hated the sight of it and what it represented. And even Molly seemed to understand what it signified, judging by the way she was lying next to it.

Sara looked up in Ryan's direction. "I'm sorry," she said, as she got up and wrapped her arms around him, pulling him close to her. "I wish I never had to let you go."

Ryan's jaw muscles clenched. "It will only be six weeks," he said, trying to sound convincing.

They were soon off to the airport, and once there, Ryan stayed with Sara as long as he could before his flight was called.

Sara stood up from her seat and hugged him close to her. "I promised myself I wasn't going to cry." She bit her lower lip in an attempt to keep it from trembling while she fought back tears.

Ryan said, "There's a note for you on your dresser."

Sara pulled away with a concerned look on her face.

"Not that kind of note," Ryan said and kissed her again. "I'll write, email, and call you every chance I can. I promise." Ryan held Sara until she looked up into his eyes. He knew there was nothing that he could say or do to make saying goodbye any easier.

Nonetheless, there was one thing he wanted her to know before he left. "I love you."

The two short weeks they'd known each other seemed like a lifetime to her, and their relationship had taken on meaning since they had met. Those three words validated everything she had felt, but had been afraid to say.

"I love you, too," she said. "Please be safe. Promise me."

"I promise."

Sara watched him go through the security gates. Suddenly he turned and pulled his left ear gently and mouthed the words "I love you" again. As he turned and walked out of sight she sat back down and cried. She tried to remember all the good times they had shared in their two short weeks together. No matter what she did, however, all she could do was picture him walking through the security checkpoint. She drove home before going to school and ran upstairs to read Ryan's note. While sitting on her bed, she noticed her hands were shaking as she opened the letter.

Dear Sara,

I love you more than I could ever imagine loving anyone in my life. The mere word, "love," does not even come close to what I feel for you. I know we just met a short time ago, but you are like a part of my soul, etched deep within my mind and heart, forever. Truthfully, I really can't even explain it. I know, here I am a writer at a loss for words, an odd predicament to say the least. With you in my life I find I look forward to each sunrise and every day I am given the chance to be here on this earth. You're the best part of my days and nights and every second in between. The other night when I stepped out onto the deck at your house, I looked at the stars in the heavens above. Off in the western sky was Venus, shining brightly among the stars. I made a wish for us. I pray I will be able to see Venus from the deserts of Iraq, because each night while I am over there, I will be looking at it and dreaming of you, sweetheart. Know that I will miss our time together, going to sleep each night while holding you in my arms, and waking up each morning with you and Molly to start a new day. As I write this letter I am still here amidst all your things. The fact is I can still smell the sweetness of your perfume. I miss you already and I am not even gone.

May the days and nights pass swiftly until we can be together again.

Love,
Ryan

Sara folded the letter and held it to her heart. Then she unfolded it and read it two more times. As she lay on the bed, she pulled Ryan's pillow close to her. The scent of his body still lingered on the pillowcase she clutched in her arms. She took a deep breath and closed her eyes, then opened them again to look at her watch.

"Hours," she said, under her breath. Mere hours was all the time that had passed since he'd left, and she had days, even weeks, to wait for his return.

Chapter Thirteen

RYAN QUICKLY APPROACHED the gate and handed his boarding pass to a uniformed female attendant. She scanned the ticket through the automated machine as Ryan unzipped his duffle bag and pulled out a postcard.

"Is there any way you could toss this into a mail drop for me?" he asked.

The attendant looked the postcard over and then glanced at Ryan's one-day-old buzz cut.

"Please," Ryan pleaded, "I should have done it before, but—"

"Sure," the attendant relented, cutting him off as she smiled at him.

Ryan boarded the plane and searched for available space in the crowded overhead compartments. A flight attendant noticed him and began doing the same. Having found room, she called out to Ryan and motioned him to come over. Ryan did so, and he managed to stow the duffle bag into a tight overhead space before finding his seat. He quickly placed his briefcase under the seat in front of him and sat down. He then buckled the seatbelt and leaned his head back. He was emotionally drained. He had a connecting flight from Boston's Logan airport to Washington's Dulles International, and from Dulles he had over six thousand miles to travel to Kuwait City, which, no matter how you sliced it, was twelve hours of flying; flying that would take him half a world away from Sara and Molly. As the plane backed away from the gate, he looked out the window and watched the other planes as they jockeyed for position on the runway.

As soon as they were airborne and had leveled off, Ryan pulled his briefcase from below the seat in front of him. It was then that he noticed a bulge in one of the inside pockets. Opening the pocket, he found a small four by six inch photo album. He pulled the tiny album from the pocket and opened it. A smile stretched across his face as he ran his fingers over the first page. Sara had written his name neatly along with hers and Molly's. Below that she wrote: "Our Story." He felt his eyes moisten and he had to blink back tears as he turned the page. The first photo was a picture of the Brant Rock beach. While the image showed nothing more than the shoreline and sky, Ryan recalled how Sara and Molly looked the very first time he watched them walk on the beach together, then the first time he held her, and later, kissed her. Across from that image Sara had placed a photo of the front view of the bed and breakfast where they had stayed in Brant Rock. Knowing the history behind the old house, particularly the fact that Sara's grandparents had built it and had lived there until their passing, Ryan found himself wishing he could have met them.

The next photo captured the backyard of the bed and breakfast with the white gazebo in the background. Ryan leaned his head back against the headrest and closed his eyes. He remembered the night that he and Sara had sat and talked after dinner with Molly at their feet. For a moment, he felt as if he was able to magically turn back the hands of time and place himself there with Sara. It wasn't until the captain turned on the "Fasten Seat Belt" light and announced that they were encountering turbulence that he was brought back to reality and remembered where he was headed. After turning the page, he saw a photo of Molly pictured by herself. Across from it was one of him and Molly playing together in Sara's backyard in Norwood. The next page revealed an image of Sara and Molly together. Ryan traced his fingers over the outline of Sara's face, and he wondered what she was doing at that very moment. A quick glance at his watch confirmed that she would be at school.

The following photos were of Sara, Jane, Jake, and Ryan at The Tower restaurant. Ryan remembered that Sara had brought her camera and had asked the waiter if he would mind taking a picture of the four of them. He smiled as he studied Jane's outfit in the photo, and then he shook his head. Even with time and photo editing, her outfit still screamed out at you when you looked at it. The rest of the album was empty except for one sentence on the first empty page where Sarah had written, "To be continued." Sara had created quite a page-turner, he thought, as he closed the album. Unable to resist the urge, he opened the album and immediately began to leaf through it again.

As the plane touched down at Dulles airport, Ryan grabbed his belongings and made his way through the terminal. A boarding call was announced for his next flight and he ran for his gate as fast as he could. He darted in between people and around a wheelchair while scanning the signs overhead, looking for his gate number. The strap on his briefcase slipped off his shoulder in the course of his mad dash. He stopped abruptly and grabbed the briefcase before it hit the floor.

"Excuse me," a woman behind him said, miffed. She was dressed in a bright red business suit, and she navigated around him in wobbly high heels as she pulled a red, wheeled travel bag behind her. Ryan shifted the briefcase and strap and took off in a run once more. A young father who was holding hands with his two toddlers on either side of him stepped out into Ryan's path. Ryan skillfully maneuvered around them and thought to himself, *For God's sake, it's like rush hour on the freeway.*

He then encountered a woman who was chatting on her cell phone while attempting to walk and pull her suitcase at the same time. She was blocking his path.

"Excuse me," Ryan said, to no avail. The woman was too busy talking on her cell phone to notice him. Like a running back who was just handed the football, Ryan looked for another way around the herd of people in front of him. First, he darted off to the left, jumping over a teenager sitting on the floor with outstretched legs and a computer in his lap. Another announcement came over the loud-speaker, this time for a flight from Dulles back to Boston. Ryan wanted nothing more than to just turn around at that very second and head back to Boston; back to Sara and Molly. It was then that he saw his gate up ahead and sprinted toward it.

Once again, there was no line in front of him, just a young uniformed airline attendant taking tickets. Ryan quickly pulled his ticket from one of the pockets in his cargo pants and handed it to her. After she ran it through the machine with a bright smile, Ryan boarded the plane. The flight was full of military contractors, soldiers, and a few members of the press, some of whom he recognized as they sat and chatted away. Ryan stashed his duffle bag overhead, took his seat, and settled in for what he already knew would be a long flight. He sat, his mind adrift, watching the screen in the seatback before him. It displayed a tiny icon of the plane as it crossed regions of the world most people only read about in newspapers or history books. Overwhelmed by exhaustion, Ryan dozed off, only to be woken suddenly when the plane encountered turbulence. He watched the tiny screen once more as the plane's flight path crossed the map and neared the Middle East.

He thought of the two amazing weeks he had just spent with Sara in Norwood. How was it, he wondered, that this woman had managed to break down every wall he had built up over the last eighteen months following his divorce? He closed his eyes and remembered the long baths they had shared with soft music playing in the background, and the way her eyes seemed to sparkle and dance in the candlelight. He soon drifted off to sleep again and dreamed of Sara. A young soldier who was seated to his left woke him when he tried to step over his legs to pass into the aisle. Still groggy from sleep, Ryan realized that he would be in Kuwait City in a few minutes, and then he would be on his way to Iraq.

Chapter Fourteen

SARA SAT DOWN AT THE kitchen table with a stack of mail piled before her and Molly curled up at her feet.

"It's been a long day, Molly girl. How was it for you, or did you sleep most of the day away?" Molly stood up wagging her tail, and then she placed her head on Sara's lap. "You miss Ryan, don't you?" Molly barked at the sound of Ryan's name. When Sara turned her attention back to her mail, Molly lay back down at Sara's feet, her head between her front paws.

"Bills, bills, and more bills," Sara said, sighing, as she sorted the mail. Bills went in one pile, junk mail off to the side, and catalogs into yet another pile. Midway through the stack in her hand, she came across a postcard with a photo of Brant Rock on the front of it. She turned it over to read the writing on the back, puzzled as to who would send her a postcard from Brant Rock.

Dear Sara,

Wish we were here. I took off one day while you

were at school and returned to Brant Rock and got this for you. I am going to try to mail this to you at the airport so you have a note from me. As the mail over here can be slow at best. I miss you and our yesterdays.

Love,
Ryan

Sara turned the postcard over in her hands and looked at the photo of Brant Rock again. She reread what Ryan wrote on the back several times. She glanced at the postmark and noticed that it was mailed from Boston on the same day he left for Iraq. Knowing they were together until his plane departed that morning, she wondered when he could have possibly had the chance to mail it.

"He's sneaky, Molly girl." Sara lowered the card down to Molly. Molly sniffed it and wagged her tail.

The following day Sara made it a point to go into school early so she could talk to the principal.

"Good morning, Sara. Come in." Principal Kline motioned her into the office with a welcoming smile.

"I know you're very busy, what with the start of the new school year and all," Sara said, as she sat down in the chair across from the desk. "But I have something very important that I wanted to talk to you about." Sara paused to collect her thoughts. "I would like to start a book drive to collect paperbacks and magazines."

"Book drive . . . ? Paperbacks . . . ?" Principal Kline sat forward in her chair.

"For our troops."

Sara shared her knowledge of what she had learned from Ryan. Plus, she had done some additional research on her own and had called a local chapter of the Blue Star Mothers the evening before, and she related all the information she had gleaned from this to Principal Kline. After a lengthy discussion, the principal agreed to allow her to start by putting a large collection box in her classroom and another one in the cafeteria. The principal even agreed to send out notes to each teacher and to the parents of every student. That evening, Sara stopped by the supermarket on her way home and picked up two large boxes. They were so large that the boy who carried them out to her car had to break them down so they would fit into her trunk. The following day she carried them both into her classroom and explained to her students what they were for.

"Ms. Ketcham, if the soldiers are reading, why can't they just come home and stop the war?" Kaitlyn asked.

"Kaitlyn, I wish they could, but it's just not that

simple," Sara replied, pausing to look at her students. They all sat listening attentively. "You see, soldiers are just like you and me. They like to read," Sara stopped, noticing Luke's raised hand.

"Yes, Luke," she said.

"I could send them my math book to read."

All the children in the classroom giggled at the thought of Luke donating his math book to the troops.

"No," Sara said, "You need to study your math book." Then she looked out at the students again. "But why don't we gather around here up front. We'll decorate these two boxes and then we can all help make signs for them."

That afternoon, when school was out, Sara took one box into the cafeteria and placed it just inside the entrance. On her way home she stopped off at the local bookstore and purchased six paperback books, three to put in each box. This would get the drive started.

Before she made dinner, Sara sat down at the antique roll top desk upstairs in the spare room. She wrote Ryan a letter telling him how excited her students grew at the idea of starting a book drive for the soldiers. As she finished addressing the envelope, she could hear the doorbell ringing downstairs, and Molly barking near the foyer. When Sara came down she found Molly wagging her tail as she stood by the front door.

"Some watchdog you are," she said to Molly, giving her a pat on the head as she unlocked the front door. After opening the door a few inches, she peered out. The sight of a person's lower torso and legs greeted her. It was a man, and he was holding a large vase of long stemmed red roses. The flowers were so abundant that the poor man's face was completely blocked from her view. She smiled, thinking to herself that he looked much like a vase with legs standing there in her doorway. Sara opened the door wide and stepped into the threshold.

A friendly voice spoke behind the roses: "I have a delivery for Ms. Sara Ketcham and Molly, the—ah—the beagle?"

"That would be us."

"Where would you like these?" the man inquired. "They're pretty heavy."

Sara motioned toward the living room table, but when the man did not move, she realized he was not able to see around the roses.

She reached out for his elbow and said, "In here, to your right. Watch your step."

The deliveryman came in, sat the flowers on the table, and pulled a ticket book out from his back pocket for her to sign. She thanked him and closed the door when he left. As she turned around, she noticed that Molly was very interested in the roses.

"Molly, we got roses!" Sara quickly opened the attached card. "They're from Ryan, sweetie, to us!" Sara said with excitement as she noticed Molly growing more interested in the flowers and vase than in what she was saying.

Molly was now standing on her two hind legs attempting to reach something in the vase. Sara turned the vase around. Much to her surprise, she found that the florist had used a bright red ribbon to carefully attach a dog biscuit and a note addressed to Molly to one of the long stemmed roses. Sara pulled the rose from the vase and read the note aloud to Molly.

"Dear Molly," Sara began, and Molly stood looking up intently and listening as Sara read. "I know I can't be there to take you for your morning walk, or play fetch in the backyard with you. Know that I miss you very much and can't wait to be home. Please enjoy this doggie cookie from me. Love, Ryan."

Sara handed the dog biscuit to Molly. Molly took the biscuit over to the throw rug and began to chew it up, thoroughly enjoying every morsel of this unexpected treat.

"Got to hand it to the guy," Sara said aloud, as she watched Molly gobble up the dog biscuit, "The man knows the way to your heart."

Sara leaned her face into the roses, closed her eyes, and inhaled their sweet fragrance.

That night, before she went to bed, she stepped outside onto the deck by herself. She pulled her jacket close around her and looked up. The sky was a black canvas etched with tiny dots of light. There above her, she found Venus, sparkling brightly. This was her favorite time of the day. Although the nights had grown colder since Ryan had left, she would often sit out on the deck looking toward Venus and talk to Ryan as though he could hear her. It somehow gave her peace.

The following morning, Sara dropped the letter off at the post office on her way to work. When she stepped into the teacher's lounge for a cup of coffee, she found that Principal Kline had already posted a letter announcing the book drive to the rest of the teaching staff. A note detailing the event would be sent home with each child later that afternoon. After she finished her coffee, Sara took three of the six books she had purchased the night before and placed them into the large collection box just inside the cafeteria door. As she turned to leave she heard a voice saying, "Thank you."

Sara turned to see Alice Young, one of the cafeteria workers.

"This is nice," Alice said, "what you are doing for the troops."

"I can only take credit for the idea. The rest is up to the school."

Alice moved closer to Sara. "My son is over there . . . in Iraq. He joined up after 9/11."

Sara noticed the worry and concern on the face of her co-worker. "Alice, I had no idea."

"He's in the Army, this is his second tour of duty over there. He loves to read." Alice gave Sara a big hug, and said, "Thank you again."

That evening after work, Sara finished up her dishes just as the phone rang.

"Hello," she said, after grabbing up the handset from the wall-mounted phone next to the fridge.

"Sweetie, have you heard anything from that cowboy of yours yet?" Jane inquired.

Sara set the dishtowel aside and leaned back against the kitchen counter. "Sort of," she said into the phone, knowing this would rile Jane up.

" 'Sort of.' What's that suppose to mean? He's been gone for days!"

"Well, I received a postcard from Brant Rock and—"

"Brant Rock," Jane interrupted, "Sweetie, Brant Rock is nowhere near Iraq."

"Jane, he drove down there and picked one up before he left and mailed it from the airport."

"And . . . ?"

"Molly and I received two dozen beautiful red

roses and a doggie biscuit from him."

Sara went on to explain how large the vase was and how the florist had meticulously tied a dog biscuit to one of the long stemmed roses just for Molly. They both laughed when Sara told her how the deliveryman had read the card.

Jane chatted away about Max and the cold front that was headed toward New England. Sara told Jane about her new book drive project she had started at her school for the troops. Jane said that she or her firm would be willing to pick up the tab when the time came to ship the books over to Iraq.

After she hung up the phone, Sara wrote another letter to Ryan. She spent the rest of the evening on the deck, looking up at the stars and thinking about him, before going to bed.

Chapter Fifteen

A SMALL CROWD OF PEOPLE HAD gathered in front of an old hotel in Baghdad.

Ryan tried to make out what was going on from across the street. Given the distance and the sun in his eyes, however, he was unable to do so. Judging by the sounds of the lighthearted laughter coming from that direction, he assumed that the gathering was a celebration of some kind.

It was only mid-morning, yet the temperature was steadily inching its way up to a predicted 103 degrees. Ryan wiped the sweat from his forehead with the back of his hand. He was glad he had remembered to apply an ample layer of sunscreen to his face, neck, and forearms before he left his room this morning.

Al, Ryan's friend and colleague of five years, walked beside him. Al had lugged his camera gear and traced Ryan's footsteps to every corner of the world in order to add images to Ryan's filed news reports. They were an odd couple to say the least. Al, Ryan figured, probably drank nearly eighty percent of all the Dr. Pepper that was produced in the world. No matter where they were, be it a postmodern Central American city or remote desert outpost in the Middle East, that was Al's drink of choice. In fact, Al swore that Dr. Pepper had medicinal properties. If the man got a cut, he would douse it with Dr. Pepper.

Ryan and Al continued to walk toward the old hotel, passing vacant, burned out buildings with boarded up windows. If it wasn't for the destruction surrounding them, one could mistake Al for a tourist, with his signature, floral Hawaiian shirt.

"You mentioned you went back to New England again," Al said, as he searched through one of the pockets of his cargo pants. "I should have gone with you and shot some photos of the leaves changing colors."

In that instant, Ryan's thoughts quickly drifted to Sara and the wonderful time they'd spent together.

Due to Ryan's lack of response, Al moved on to another subject. "Did I mention that little hottie I met? What was her name. . . ?" Al said, as he snapped his fingers in an attempt to recall the woman's name.

"It was either Cheryl or Carol," Ryan interjected, "And yes, you mentioned it. Twice. But who's counting. You're like a hormone on two feet, buddy."

Al looked over at Ryan, who was scratching a two-day growth of beard on his face. Ryan seemed different since he came back to work, almost distracted. He was just not himself, and Al wasn't sure why. But he was certain he would get to the bottom of what was bothering Ryan.

"Earth to Ryan . . ." Al joked.

Just as Al placed his hand on Ryan's shoulder to get his attention, an old red car with a dented trunk rattled up the street with a single male occupant behind the wheel. The old car sped by them, heading straight toward the crowd across the street. Suddenly it exploded in a ball of fire. Al pushed Ryan to the ground, screaming, "Get down!"

Flames shot up from the suicide bomber's car, engulfing both it and the front entrance of the hotel. Dust, smoke, and debris filled the air, along with the screams and cries of the injured.

"Welcome back to our world, Spence," Al said, scrambling to his feet.

He grabbed a small camera that he always carried in his pants pocket and began filming the scene.

Ryan sat on the ground, covered in dust and debris. He rubbed his eyes as he watched Al busy at work. No matter how long Ryan had done this job, he could never get used to the stench of death that now filled the air.

"You okay?" Al yelled over the sounds of the screams and approaching sirens.

He turned back to Ryan, taking his sight from the eyepiece of his camera. Within seconds, the street began to fill with police and military.

AFTER TYPING UP HIS article that night, Ryan connected his computer to his satellite phone to file his report. As he sat and waited for the data transmission to complete, he wondered for the first time in his career why he was there, a civilian in a war zone. He began musing to himself, considering what he would do for a living if he ever left his post as a journalist. Having come up blank, he took out a notepad and pen and started a letter to Sara, but his thoughts were interrupted when a young journalist entered the barracks.

"They, uh . . . said . . ." Nervous and stammering, the young journalist began again: "They said I could bunk with you guys."

Ryan looked up at a scrawny youth in fatigues. "Sure. There's a cot over there." Ryan pointed and the kid walked over to the cot with his gear.

"If you wanted five-star accommodations, they're two doors down on the right," Ryan joked, as he looked over at the kid.

The journalist gave a half-hearted, nervous laugh.

"Your first time over here?" Ryan asked.

"Uh huh." He set his gear down with a thud.

Al looked up from his cot and stared at the newcomer. "Hey kid, ya think you can keep it down? I'm trying to get some sleep," he grumbled and turned over in his cot.

"Don't mind him," Ryan said, looking over at Al. "A land mine could go off and he'd sleep right through it."

"Land mine?" The kid's eyes widened.

Upon hearing the cot squeak as the young journalist sat down, Al said, "Yeah, Princess, like the one that's under your cot."

The kid jumped up.

"Sit down. Don't mind Al over there," Ryan said. He stood up and extended his hand to the youth. "He gets cranky when he doesn't get his beauty rest. Ryan Spencer, by the way," Ryan said, introducing himself before pointing toward Al's cot. "The grumpy one over there is Al. He's more of a morning person, if you know what I mean."

"Carl. My name's Carl Miller," the kid said, as he dug through his equipment bag, in search of something.

Ryan peered down at the contents of the bag then walked over to his own gear to grab a package of baby wipes. "Here." Ryan tossed the package to

Carl from across the room.

"Baby wipes. What am I suppose to do with these?" Carl looked back at Ryan with a confused look on his face. "I don't think I'm going to be changing diapers out there."

"Have you checked yours lately?" Al, clearly irritated, remarked sarcastically.

Ryan shook his head. "They're best for getting the dust off your skin and for easy clean up when you're out in the field. Plus, they're great for wiping dust off your gear."

"Ladies! P-l-e-a-s-e, can the sisterhood exchange cleaning ideas tomorrow over tea?"

Ryan turned his attention back to the notepad and pen in front of him and finished his letter to Sara. Once he sealed the letter up, he tucked it into his pocket to mail from the base in the morning. He stepped outside into the darkness and looked overhead at the Middle Eastern sky. It was here, under the stars, that he felt closest to Sara. After locating the planet Venus, his memories of what they had shared swept through his mind. Try as he might, he could not recall ever taking the time to look up at the night sky when he had been over here before. He closed his eyes and recalled how soft Sara's skin felt; like velvet under his fingertips. He inhaled a breath of air and, for a second, he could almost smell the sweet scent of her hair.

Chapter Sixteen

IT WAS ONE HOUR PAST the time Sara would normally have headed home. While her attention was needed for many of the tasks, some could either have waited or simply been taken home to be completed. After placing the last spelling test on the stack she had already graded, she leaned back and looked at the clock on the wall. She knew full well what she was doing; she had even talked about it with Jane the week before. She was avoiding going home. Work was a distraction; an escape from what was haunting her.

She found that if she left work at the usual time, she would inevitably turn on the evening news. But instead of just listening to it as it played in the background while she prepared dinner for Molly and herself as she used to do, she would now sit almost paralyzed with fear in front of the television set. Every time a scene from the Middle East filled the screen, she would instinctively grab the remote and turn up the volume. She hated that. But why on earth did she do this? Did she somehow think that by turning up the volume she could change the outcome of the death toll, or assure Ryan's safety?

Sleep, which was once a sweet distraction from the daily grind, and from missing Ryan, now involved nothing but nightmares. It all started shortly after they aired a segment on the news about a prominent journalist and his crew who had been badly injured in Iraq following an attack on their convoy. That night, as she slept, Sara replayed the images of the newscast over and over again, until the slain journalist being put into a body bag became Ryan. As the medic began to zip the bag closed, Ryan reached his hand out to her. "Help me, Sara," he pleaded. "Help me."

"No!" Sara screamed out as she sat up in bed, crying and shaking uncontrollably, and waking Molly in the process. She knew it was only a dream, but found herself unable to go back to sleep. From that point on, Sara started avoiding the news, as though that act itself would keep Ryan safe.

❧

SHE GATHERED UP HER things as she prepared to leave the classroom. She glanced over at the box for the book drive and noted that it was almost full with books and magazines. This was the second time in two weeks. She and Jane had already boxed up a large shipment and sent it off to the troops. She turned around and leaned against the classroom wall, then tilted her head back and closed her eyes. God, how her life had changed since she met Ryan. Before Ryan, she lived an almost sheltered life. War and civil unrest in another country was just that: in another country. She hated war, had never even liked movies that depicted it. She never understood why grown adults simply could not work out their differences with words. Why in God's name did it have to always turn to blood-shed?

She had recently formed a kinship with several military wives and their families. The first time she mentioned IEDs in a conversation with Jane, the poor woman thought she was talking about a new form of birth control. It was while she was explaining that an IED was not a new breakthrough contraceptive on the market—rather it was a military acronym used for "improvised explosive device"—that Sara realized she was able to relate more easily to people with loved ones serving in the military. Nevertheless, she missed Ryan beyond words. He wrote to her every day, but that only resulted in a handful of letters, five postcards, and a dozen or so emails—not to mention a few phone calls and the roses he had sent to her and Molly—but it wasn't the same. She felt a twinge of guilt for wanting more. Nonetheless, she was thankful that Ryan was in her life. In fact, it was hard to imagine life without him now. In a few days he would be back in Norwood; back in her arms, home, safe.

She turned off the classroom lights and locked the door behind her. When she got home, she immediately gathered the mail and went through it to see if there was a letter or card from Ryan. To her delight she found one and set it aside without opening it. Molly had to be fed first. After that task was accomplished, Sara sat down to a light pasta salad and read the letter from Ryan.

Dear Sara,

It has been hell over here. There is so much more than the war itself these days, but enough of my complaining. I miss you, sweetheart. When I first came over here I was counting the weeks till my return. Then it was down to days, now I am counting the hours and seconds. I guess what I am alluding to is quite simple to say but difficult to figure out. I have tried to talk this over with Al and I think you know how he responded. The fact is, Sara, I want to leave my position with the Post. That said, I have nothing to follow that up with. If I stay with the Post and request another assignment they would most likely send me off to another place far from Norwood; far from you and Molly. So, I guess what I am saying is that I want to quit. Not sure what I would do if I did? What I am sure of is that it will take time for them to replace me. Anyway, enough of that.

I wonder sometimes how lucky it was for us to have found each other on the beaches of Brant Rock. I know we haven't known each other all that long, but deep down inside I feel like I have known you all my life. I know now that a part of me was missing; there was a void in my life before I met you. In fact, after looking back, I realize that I always felt that way. You fill the emptiness within my soul. Could it be we are what some people call "soul mates?" You are the missing piece of a puzzle within my life, which I have been searching for all along.

As I write this letter to you, I know no matter what words I put upon the page, I can never truly express how much I need and love you. May your heart be able to read between the lines and understand what I can't seem to find words to say.

Love,
Ryan

Sara let out a heavy sigh as she looked up from the letter. She knew Ryan was right. She had felt something different from the moment she opened her heart up to him. There was more to Ryan than mere words could describe. She knew she felt the same way as Ryan; that an integral part of her soul was missing. Jane was always gabbing away about this New Age stuff, which Sara had never understood. Could she have been right all along? Sara thought about this as she took the letter upstairs and added it to the stack of letters on her dresser.

She also dwelled on Ryan's thoughts concerning a career change. In a way, she felt as though a heavy weight had been lifted from her. But was he doing this for her? Would he end up resenting her later for giving up a career that he loved? She only wanted him home, safe, and with her. Her emotions were a mixture of happiness—in that someday they would not be thousands of miles apart—and guilt, realizing that it meant Ryan would have to make a career change.

She stood thinking about all this until the doorbell rang. She quickly ran downstairs and opened the front door a crack. To her surprise, Russ was standing on the doorstep.

"Can I come in?" Russ waited for her to open the door. "I really need to talk to you."

Sara opened the door reluctantly. Russ entered the house and bent down to pet Molly. Sara noticed the disappointment displayed on Russ' face after Molly moved away from him to stand next to her.

"Can I get you a cup of coffee?" Sara asked as Russ took a seat on the couch.

He unbuttoned the top button on his shirt and loosened his tie. "That would be nice, thank you."

Sara went into the kitchen, wondering what on earth they needed to talk about after all these months.

"Molly." Sara heard Russ calling the dog. She looked down and saw that Molly had followed her into the kitchen, refusing to go to Russ. Molly returned to the living room only when Sara went back and handed the coffee to Russ.

"How have you been?" Russ inquired, watching Molly stare at him like a stranger.

"What is it you need?" Sara asked curtly.

"Sara, I think I made a mistake."

" 'A mistake?' " Sara echoed his words.

"I should have never left you, Sara." He set his cup down on the coffee table and stood up. He paced nervously in front of the fireplace, waiting for Sara's response.

Sara sat in the chair across from Russ in disbelief. At first she said nothing while she attempted to process this new information.

"No. You should have never had an affair. Your leaving was simply the next step."

"Please, I'm sorry," Russ said, taking his seat again.

Sara sat forward in her chair, angry now. "When you decided to have your affair, you had a choice. Was I given one? No, I wasn't! You thought of yourself. You made that choice for both of us."

Russ hung his head and clasped his hands together. All he could do was look down at the floor. While he continued to do this, he said, "I love you, Sa—"

Sara shook her head in disbelief and cut him off sharply. "Russ, I loved you. I was a faithful wife to you and it didn't matter."

Following those words, they both sat in silence for several minutes.

"My grandmother always told me that anyone can fall in love," Sara said. "The trick is to fall in love over and over again, especially when times get tough." She glared at Russ, who held his gaze on her.

"When two people are married," she continued to say, "day-to-day living is hard. There are two personalities under one roof, bills to be paid, and decisions to be made. More importantly, a marriage has an emotional bank account."

" 'Emotional bank account?' " Russ questioned.

"You're a financial wizard, Russ. You do the math."

Russ continued to sit with a confused look on his face, which forced Sara to elaborate. "Russ, if you're not nurturing a relationship, you're simply taking away from it. What you did to us—to me, with your affair—caused an emotional bankruptcy."

Sara felt great relief from expressing her true feelings. For months she had kept silent about what had happened between them.

"Sara, this sounds like some crap Jane's been feeding you. 'Emotional bank account.' " Russ shook his head, trying to downplay all that he had done.

Sara stood up and picked up the empty coffee cup. "I think you should go."

Russ stood up as well, and said, "I've changed. Please give us another chance."

Sara opened the front door and turned toward Russ. "You had your chance, and there is no 'us.' Not anymore."

After he was gone, she sat down again. She looked at the empty coffee cup in her hand and realized that her feelings for Russ were just as empty.

TWO DAYS LATER, SHE drove to Boston Logan airport. She found herself standing in the very spot she stood when Ryan left six weeks ago. She glanced at her watch again and again as though that would make his flight arrive sooner. Watching people scurry back and forth like ants, both young and old, all coming or going, she felt like a voyeur of sorts as she witnessed hugs, kisses, and tears. Even in a crowded airport she could easily spot couples who were reuniting. Once their eyes met, the love from their hearts was conveyed through their eyes.

She waited for Ryan among the crowds. Each time a plane arrived she felt her heart pounding with anticipation as she searched the nameless faces of passengers walking from the arrival gate. One hour and forty minutes after his flight was due in, she spotted Ryan. He looked exhausted. His dark brown hair had grown out, his face was drawn, and it looked like he had lost at least fifteen pounds. Sara could not wait one more minute, so she ran toward him.

"Ryan," she said, her voice cracking as tears of joy ran down her cheeks.

Ryan turned and stopped. He dropped his duffle bag to the floor and pulled her close to him. In his hand was a single red rose he had picked up in the Dulles airport gift shop.

Chapter Seventeen

After unlocking the side door to the house, Sara and Ryan stepped inside as Molly bounded across the kitchen floor to greet them, happily wagging her tail. Ryan placed his duffle bag on the floor and bent down to her.

He scratched the back of her neck and asked, "Did you miss me?"

Sara laughed. The movement of Molly's swaying tail made her whole body wiggle. Molly's display of affection toward Ryan was in complete contrast to the greeting she gave Russ last night.

Ryan looked up at Sara and asked, "Would you mind if I took a shower?"

"Go ahead. I have clean towels out upstairs. While you do that I'll fix us something to eat."

Sara turned, but before she could walk away Ryan grabbed her gently around the waist. Their eyes met. "Hey, lady. I missed you," he said, before kissing her.

"I missed you, too. Now go get cleaned up."

Ryan quickly took his duffle bag upstairs, stripped off his clothes, and turned on the shower as he got in the tub.

Sara set the oven to 400 degrees and took two pieces of chicken out of the refrigerator. While the oven was being preheated, she poured some Italian breadcrumbs on a plate then sprinkled a little thyme, basil, garlic salt, and oregano into the breadcrumbs. She grated a small amount of Parmesan cheese over the top and mixed the dry ingredients together. Next, she cut them into long strips. She then coated the chicken strips in olive oil and rolled the chicken in the dry ingredients. Just as she put the chicken into the oven she heard the shower running upstairs.

For the first five minutes Ryan closed his eyes and enjoyed the feeling of the luxurious warm water cascading over his body. The shower almost had a healing sensation, as though it cleansed not only his body, but also the harrowing experiences from the last six weeks in Iraq.

He lifted his face and let the water rush over it. Suddenly he felt Sara's arms wrap around him from behind. They said nothing to each other as she gently washed his shoulders and back, and then she reached around him and began to wash his chest. Ryan slowly turned to face her, and kissed her passionately on the lips before making his way down to her neck.

Their pent up desire was erased as they made

love in the shower and then again before they fell asleep that night, wrapped in each other's arms with Molly curled up beside the bed. The following morning, Ryan woke up before Sara and quickly went downstairs to feed Molly. Following that, he scrambled some eggs and also made some bacon and biscuits he found in the refrigerator. He was pouring coffee when he heard Sara's footsteps slowly descending the stairs.

Sara entered the kitchen wiping sleep from her eyes.

"Hey, sleepyhead," Ryan said. "You up for some breakfast? Molly and I have been very busy."

Sara looked around the kitchen. "I can see that," she said, hugging him. "I wish I didn't have to go to work this morning." Sara took a seat as Ryan set a plate down in front of her. "Mmm . . . smells good."

"Two more days and we'll be off to Albuquerque, where we can spend five whole days together. No work, nothing but you and me, together, alone." Ryan reached across the table and caressed her hand.

"I can't wait for Wednesday!" Sara exclaimed, taking another bite of eggs and a sip of coffee. "Your travel agent sent a next day package. It's on the foyer table."

"It must be our travel itinerary, and I asked her to include some information about New Mexico for you." Ryan used his biscuit to gather up the last of his eggs.

"What do I need with that? I have you as my own personal travel guide." Sara smiled and drained the last drop of coffee from her cup. She rose and carried her dishes over to the sink. "Mr. Spencer, a woman could get v-e-r-y used to having you around all the time."

ON WEDNESDAY MORNING, THEY took quick showers, grabbed their packed suitcases, and headed for the airport. Two layovers and a few hours later, Sara stepped out of the aircraft at the Albuquerque Sunport. After they secured a Toyota Camry from the car rental company, they were greeted by a beautiful, clear blue sky and large majestic mountains. Sara was mesmerized. Ryan headed north on I-25 to their hotel.

"It is so different here, so . . . spread out," Sara remarked, looking out the car window at the long ribbon of highway that stretched out before them.

"Look." Ryan leaned forward, pointing up at two brightly colored hot air balloons floating against the picture perfect blue canvas above them.

In a half hour Ryan pulled up to the hotel entrance. A friendly doorman opened Sara's car door and extended a hand to help her out. After they checked into their room, Sara called Jane to see how Molly was doing. When she was through with the call, they both showered and dressed, as Ryan had plans for dinner. They eventually headed east in the Camry and stopped when they arrived at the base of the Sandia Mountains.

"Come on," Ryan said, as he got out of the car.

"I thought we were going to dinner?"

"We are. At the top of the mountain."

Sara looked up at the breathtaking view of the mountain that stood some ten thousand feet, towering majestically before her. Ryan put his arm around her and led her toward a boarding area for the tram, which would take them to a restaurant located at the top of the mountain. Sara could not believe the amazing views from the tram, which slowly made its way up the 2.7 miles that comprised the total distance to the mountaintop.

"The air is so fresh up here." Sara inhaled deeply as she looked at the trees below and then out across the horizon.

Fifteen minutes later, they arrived at the top of the Sandias, and Sara immediately ran to the railing, looking in every direction.

"Ryan, this is simply . . . out of this world. Look at the city below us!" She turned to the west and added, "And the sunset." Then she took out her camera and snapped several pictures as the sun sank behind a small mountain range. The dusky blue western sky was turning bright orange mixed with the palest hues of pink.

Ryan looked at his watch. "Come on, let's eat. You hungry?"

"Starving."

That night, they dined at a beautiful, elegant restaurant that offered fine American cuisine with an amazing view of the city, which sparkled and shimmered below.

The following day they had an early breakfast at the hotel, and then they headed over to Balloon Fiesta Park. There, on the green grass, lay hundreds of colorful hot air balloons and their crew-members preparing them for flight. Just as the sun began to peek over the Sandia Mountains, hundreds of balloons lifted off in a mass ascension that dotted the sky above them. Afterwards, Sara and Ryan left the park and headed over to Old Town, where they feasted on Mexican food and visited all the shops. After a considerable amount of walking around Balloon Fiesta Park and Old Town, they decided to take a break by sitting in the Old Town Park. While a cool breeze blew, they relaxed on the bench, which was situated below an old cotton-wood tree, and admired a beautiful, old gazebo in the center of the park.

The following morning, they returned to witness

another mass ascension of balloons. This day, however, the sky was filled with special shapes, including a cow, a giant daisy, a stagecoach, and an ark filled with animals. There was even a giant can of dog food, which made Sarah smile and think of Molly.

"Look!" Ryan said, pointing up toward a bear-shaped balloon.

Once all the balloons were in the air, Ryan drove the Camry northward to Santa Fe.

"Santa Fe was founded by the Spanish in 1610," Ryan explained. "It's our state's capitol, and was originally called the Royal City of the Holy Faith."

"I didn't know that."

Ryan pulled into the plaza area and parked the car. They walked around the plaza hand-in-hand, visiting all the little shops and vendors. On the edge of the plaza, Ryan stopped in front of an old chapel.

"There are several mysteries that surround this chapel," Ryan told her before they entered. "It was built and completed in 1878. The sisters, however, had no access to the choir loft. If I remember correctly, it's about twenty or so feet above the chapel floor. To add to this dilemma, when we go in you'll see that the overall chapel is very small. The sisters contacted several carpenters in the area, but the only solution they could offer was to put in a steep staircase that would lead up to the choir loft.

While that would give them access, it would also take away from the overall floor space and sitting area."

Sara stood listening to Ryan intently.

He continued. "The sisters prayed, and asked for guidance from St. Joseph, who is the patron saint of carpenters. Legend has it that on the ninth day of prayer a man came to the chapel seeking work. Equipped with only a donkey and a toolbox, the man worked for months constructing a magnificent spiral staircase for the sisters. However, after the staircase was finished he disappeared without pay or even a thank you."

"Just vanished?" Sara asked.

"Gone without a trace. The sisters were bewildered, and they searched high and low for the man. They even ran an ad in an attempt to find him. Nevertheless, all their efforts yielded nothing. Today, some people still believe St. Joseph himself answered the sisters' prayers. Thus, some referred to the staircase as 'St. Joseph's Staircase.'

"That in itself is quite a mystery. The fact is, however, that the staircase was said to be innovative for the time period, given its mere design."

"How so?" Sara inquired.

"The staircase was constructed without the use of any nails."

"No nails?" Sara was no carpenter, but a structure like the one Ryan described had to at least have nails or something to hold it together. "Then how is it held together?"

"The staircase makes not one, but two 360 degree turns. Remember, I told you the chapel was small inside. The turns and the spiral design take up a very small footprint. But only wooden pegs were used, without the use of glue. There's no support from the walls. Therefore, this staircase basically stands without any means of visible support.

"Are we allowed to go inside?"

"Sure."

Ryan and Sara went inside the old chapel, which was filled with tourists. Sara walked over to the old staircase and found that it was just as Ryan had described, spiraling up to the choir loft. The craftsmanship was amazing. Sara snapped several photos to show her class. Ryan stood back and allowed her to look around. Sara walked over to the altar. As she stood there, she turned to Ryan briefly and smiled. He was still amazed by how beautiful she was. For a moment, he found himself envisioning her standing there in a white wedding gown with a train flowing around her feet.

"Excuse me." An elderly woman bumped into him. Having noticed Ryan's line of sight, and the way he and Sara looked at each other, she said, "Oh, your wife is so beautiful. You two must still be newlyweds."

"Newlyweds?" Ryan was taken aback when the elderly woman hugged him. "God bless you both." She turned and left.

Sara came over to Ryan, and asked, "Who was that?"

"I have no idea. She thought we were married." Ryan turned to look for the woman, but she had vanished from sight.

At lunchtime, he took Sara to a restaurant he knew, which was off the beaten path. It was so out of the way, he guessed that many of the Santa Fe locals didn't even know of its existence. The waiter took them upstairs and seated them next to a fireplace. The atmosphere and food were wonderful. Sara asked the waiter to take a photo of the two of them in front of the fireplace.

After the waiter handed the camera back to Sara, she and Ryan sat down at their table. Ryan leaned forward with a serious expression. "Sara, I need to talk to you."

"Is everything okay?" Sara asked, a concerned look replacing her smile.

"Yes and no." Ryan stopped speaking as he gathered his thoughts. "I want to quit my job."

"Ryan—" Sara reached across the table and

gently laid her hand on his.

He interrupted, "Sara, please understand that this is something I've been thinking about for the last few weeks."

"Is this because of me?" Sara questioned. "Ryan, I don't want you to end up resenting me later because you left a career you loved."

Ryan took Sara's hand. "Technically, I guess you could say it's because of you." Ryan hesitated. "However, it's really due to the love I feel for you and for us."

"Are you sure this is what you really want to do?"

"Very. The only thing I'm unsure of is what I'm going to do after I quit."

"I talked to Jane about this when you wrote to me and told me you were thinking about it. She said she would be happy to pass your résumé along to several clients of hers."

"Jane would do that?" Ryan inquired in a shocked tone. "For me?"

"You bet."

Ryan and Sara finished eating and headed back to Albuquerque. The following day, they visited the cemetery, where Ryan placed flowers on the graves of both of his parents. After that, he showed Sara where his father's cattle ranch was located, which, like most parts of the country, was now mostly subdivided for homes. The house where Ryan had grown up was still standing, and looked pretty much unchanged as he drove past it. That evening they met with a handful of Ryan's closest friends for dinner.

The following day, they returned to Boston and Ryan began preparing for his trip back to Iraq. On Tuesday afternoon, he placed a call to his boss at *The Post*.

"Steve. Ryan Spencer." He took a deep breath and thought about what he was doing. He and Sara had talked about it and he knew what he was doing was right. Right for him and right for them.

"Hey, Ryan." Ryan could hear all the noise in the background from the newsroom just as Steve said, "I have to tell you, your last few articles featuring our men and woman serving over there, and not just focusing on the war, were really well received. Well done."

"Steve, there's something I need to tell you."

"Sure, what's on your mind?"

Ryan sat at the kitchen table, nervously doodling on a piece of paper. "Steve, this will be my last six weeks with *The Post*. That should give you ample time to get another journalist to replace me in the field."

"It's *The Times*, isn't it? Did they make you a better offer?" He could hear Steve closing his office door, which caused the background noise to cease.

"Tell you what, we'll meet or beat it, son."

"There's no offer. My resignation letter is in the mail to you, but I wanted to tell you personally."

"No offer?" Steve cleared his throat. "You just need some time off. When was the last time you used your vacation days?"

"Steve, it's not that." Ryan hesitated, collecting his thoughts. "I met someone and I just do not want to be gone so much anymore, or be so far away."

"But you're still putting in your six weeks with us . . . right?"

"I fly out of Boston on Sunday. That should give you enough time to fill my position."

After the call, Ryan felt as though a weight had been lifted from him. While he liked his boss, and felt bad for leaving, he knew deep down in his heart that it was the right thing to do.

That evening, Sara and Ryan met Jane and Jake at the Tower for dinner again. Ryan announced that he had tendered his resignation to *The Post*.

"This calls for a toast," Jane said, lifting up her glass. "I want your résumé emailed over to my office in the morning." She dug through her bright red handbag and found a business card, which she handed to him across the table.

"I still have six weeks over there—"

Jane cut him off. "Sweetie, you let me take care

of this. Just get your résumé over to me."

❧

RYAN QUICKLY UPDATED his résumé and emailed it to Jane. With that taken care of, he glanced through the local phone book and found the number of a local florist, which he jotted down on a piece of paper. Since he would be spending another six weeks in Iraq, he wanted his last night with Sara to be memorable. He planned each detail and made a list so that he wouldn't forget anything.

Upon returning home, he carried a large bag of rose petals and a bottle of champagne into the house. After putting the champagne in the refrigerator, he carried a vase of long stemmed roses to the foyer and placed it on a small table against the wall. Molly, feeling his excitement, followed his every step, wagging her tail all the while.

Ryan stood back and looked at the roses. "What d'ya think, Molly?"

Molly barked.

"I'll take that as a yes," Ryan said, petting Molly on the head.

Ryan grabbed the bag of rose petals from the refrigerator and began to scatter the rose petals up the stairway and in the bedroom. He heard a noise behind him and turned to find Molly attempting to get rose petals off her tongue and from the roof of her mouth. She resembled someone who had just consumed a large quantity of peanut butter as she stood before him making a smacking sound.

"Come here. You're not supposed to eat them Molly," Ryan told her, trying not to laugh as he removed several rose petals from her mouth. Realizing that Molly was being just a little too helpful, he decided to block the stairs with a child safety gate before continuing to lay the rose petals on the stairway. He then carefully arranged the remaining rose petals on the bed in the shape of a heart and placed a long stemmed rose on the pillow.

After going back downstairs, he found an ice bucket in Sara's cupboard. He put the champagne into the bucket, and added some ice to keep it chilled. Next, he found two champagne flutes and carried them upstairs, along with the ice bucket. An old-fashioned checkered tablecloth he'd found at the store was then spread out on the floor. When that was done, he lined the bathtub with more rose petals and placed candles around the edge of the tub itself. As a final touch he turned on some soft music. Satisfied with everything he had done, he made his way downstairs carefully, so as not to disturb the rose petals on the stairway.

Finally, he prepared a light dinner in the kitchen. His timing was perfect; he heard Molly bark, which announced Sara's return home from work, just as he put the meal in the oven to keep it warm.

Sara entered the kitchen and took in the aroma of the roasted chicken that filled the air. She greeted Ryan with a kiss. "Mmm, something smells good."

"Want to have a picnic with me?" Ryan asked, with a boyish grin.

"It's not even 40 degrees outside!"

Ryan set the plates down and helped her off with her coat. Sara glanced around Ryan. She saw the roses on the table in the foyer, and walked over and smelled them.

"They smell beautiful. Thank you," she said.

"Why don't you go upstairs? I'll be there in a few minutes."

Sara turned to go up the stairs and noticed the rose petals leading up the stairway.

"Hmmm. . . . Molly, do you know anything about this? I thought I told you that you were in charge today. You know you have to keep a close eye on him."

Molly wagged her tail and followed Sara up the path of rose petals. Ryan neatly arranged the food on two plates and climbed the stairway. He found Sara in the bedroom in tears. Ryan set the two dinner plates on the dresser and held her in his arms. "Hey, this is supposed to make you happy."

"It does." Sara wiped tears from her cheek.

"Then why are you crying?"

"They're happy tears," she replied, as she sniffled.

"Those would be different from, say, the sad ones, I hope?"

Sara laughed and picked up the long stemmed rose from the pillow. "Thank you. Has anyone ever told you how wonderful you are?"

"Molly, but that was after I had to help her get some rose petals out of her mouth."

Sara laughed as she pictured both Ryan and Molly spreading the rose petals throughout the house.

Ryan smiled and then picked up their plates. They sat down together on the checkered tablecloth on the bedroom floor.

"A picnic, even in 40 degree weather," he said. "Just for you."

Ryan reached for the champagne, popped the cork on the bottle, and poured them each a glass. Then they ate dinner as they sat on the floor. Afterwards, they made love and took a candlelight bath together.

Chapter Eighteen

SARA MOVED ABOUT THE house helping Ryan gather his things for his trip back to Iraq. She wasn't enthusiastic about it, and therefore her actions reminded her of her students. Whenever they had to do something they didn't want to do, they did so halfheartedly; simply going through the motions. She knew Ryan had to complete his last six-week assignment over in Iraq. Nonetheless, knowing this and getting her body to actually cooperate was an entirely different thing. She felt as though she was moving in slow motion. The more Ryan glanced at his wristwatch to check the time before they drove to the airport, the worse it became.

"Darn it!" Ryan cursed, as he searched frantically through the pockets of his cargo pant.

Sara looked up. "What's wrong?"

"It's got to be here . . . somewhere." Ryan turned quickly and ran upstairs, then returned a few minutes later. He looked through his briefcase and took out his notepad, computer, and even the photo album Sara had made for him. "Where did I put it?"

Sara walked over to him and put a hand on his shoulder. "Babe, what is it?"

"My silver dollar."

"Did you look in that dish on the dresser where you always put your change at night?"

"Yes," he answered. Flustered, he continued to search through every pocket in his briefcase a second time. Finding nothing, he quickly stood up and turned his attention back to his pants pockets.

Sara looked at her wristwatch. "You're going to miss your flight. I'll look for it tonight."

"You don't understand." Ryan stooped down and began digging through his duffle bag. "It's a 1927 Peace Dollar."

"That silver dollar you always carry with your change?"

"Yes. It was my great-grandfather's. His mother gave it to him when he served in World War ll. When my grandpa was drafted and went overseas during the Korean War, his father then passed it along to him, who then gave it to my father, who served in the Vietnam War."

"Ryan, I have a safety deposit box at the bank for things like that. We should have put it in there for safekeeping. My God, something as sentimental and valuable as that should have been put away."

Ryan looked up from his duffle bag. "Sara, that's just the point. It was for my safety . . . to give me luck." Turning his attention back to his duffle bag, he laid the contents out on the floor.

Suddenly, Sara understood the significance of the silver dollar. Ryan glanced at his wristwatch. Realizing that they had to leave for the airport, he stuffed everything back into the duffle bag in haste.

When they arrived at the airport, Sara and Ryan sat together just outside the security gate. Sara fidgeted with her purse strap while crossing and uncrossing her legs. Ryan knew she was under a lot of stress but was trying very hard to hide it from him.

He hugged her. "I'll only be gone six weeks," he said, trying to reassure her that everything would be okay.

The first time Ryan had left on assignment to Iraq, Sara thought she knew what to expect. However, she now knew how naïve she had been. She hated the thought of him being in such a volatile region of the world. She tried to take solace in the fact that Ryan's resignation letter was now in the hands of his boss and this would be his final assignment in Iraq. *It's just six weeks*, she told herself, *that's all*. Why then could she not just focus on that rather than dwell on the danger?

"Sara, you okay?" Ryan asked, after she had grown silent.

"I just wish you weren't going to . . ." Sara

realized she could not even say the word, "Iraq." Not wanting Ryan to remember her this way, she tried to gather all her strength together and reassert herself. "I don't want you to go." Sara closed her eyes, fighting back the tears.

"I don't either." He gently brushed a lock of her hair away from her forehead. "I want so badly to be everything to you, and when I come home—"

Sara smiled, interrupting him. "You already are."

Ryan looked at his watch again and rose to his feet. "I'm sorry but . . . it's time."

"I know." Sara stood up reluctantly. She knew he had to have ample time to make his way through the security area and get to his gate. "Why can't this be six weeks from now with you coming home and not leaving?"

Ryan simply could not respond. The words seemed to be lodged in the back of his throat. Finally he said, "I have to go. I love you." Then he took her into his arms and kissed her.

Sara leaned back, still holding him tightly in her arms, and looked deep into his eyes. "Ryan Spencer, I love you, too!"

Ryan pulled away reluctantly, then picked up his duffle bag and briefcase. He started for the security checkpoint, but as he did so, he turned to face her several times, pulling his left ear while mouthing the words "I love you."

Ryan flew his same route from Boston Logan to Dulles, where he boarded a flight to Kuwait City. During the flight, he talked to a young sergeant from Fort Bragg, North Carolina for several hours—the officer had taken the window seat next to him. Upon his arrival in Kuwait, Al met him at the airport.

"What the hell is this? I hear you're resigning?" Al asked.

"And how are you doing, Al?" Ryan asked as he hoisted the strap of his briefcase up onto his shoulder.

"Fine. Now did you turn in your resignation or not?"

"I see Steve wasted no time in breaking the news to everyone."

Al shook his head. "Four months! That's all I'll give you! F-o-u-r months, and you'll miss it!"

Ryan looked around as a tank rolled by. "Yep . . . there is so much to miss here."

"You know what I mean. Your adrenaline pumping, chasing that next article, getting off to—"

"Al," Ryan interrupted. "I'm going to ask Sara to marry me when I get home. I picked out an engagement ring. In fact, it's been paid for and is sitting in the jeweler's safe in Boston as we speak."

"Marry her! E-a-r-t-h to Ryan, did you forget what Ann did to you?"

"That was Ann. Sara's different."

"You're crazy! You go out and purchase a couple of left hand rings and play house for a couple of years." Al's face reddened with anger. "This is your career you're tossing away!"

Ryan kept walking. While he understood Al's concerns about his career, something in Al's tone made him wonder if there was something more bothering him.

Al kept it going, saying, "Don't do it! You're going to regret it."

Al stepped in front of Ryan and blocked his path. The two men looked each other in the eye.

"This is what I want," Ryan said.

"You're going to hate it, Spence."

"Where did you get such a rosy disposition?" Ryan asked rhetorically, laughing as he patted Al on the back. Ryan decided to change the subject, asking, "What's been going on here?"

"There was a bus bombing in Baghdad yesterday. Everyone onboard was killed."

"Did you get any footage?"

"Wasn't here yet. The rookie kid . . . what's his name. . . ?"

"Carl?"

"Yeah, that's it. Anyway, he told me about it."

After a night in Kuwait and some much-needed rest, both Ryan and Al boarded a plane for

Baghdad International Airport. Armed with bottles of water to keep hydrated, and donning their military flack vests and helmets, they no longer looked like two employees heading off to work. Once on the ground in Baghdad, Ryan could hear echoes of what appeared to be distant thunder. He knew all too well that the sound was not thunder at all. *Miss this work*, he thought to himself. *Why?*

Ryan watched as the bomb-sniffing dogs inspected the pile of duffle bags and luggage. One of the dogs stopped and looked in Ryan's direction. For a second, Ryan pictured Molly with a rose petal stuck to her tongue. He thought back on their last night together: the rose petals on the stairway; in the bedroom and bathroom; the candlelight bath. . . . Ryan glanced at his watch as thoughts of Sara flooded his mind.

Both Ryan and Al boarded the shuttle. After taking his seat, Ryan watched as a Humvee armed with a machine gun took up the forward position to escort the shuttle. He mused to himself, thinking what it would be like to go to work someday without needing a machine-gun-toting Humvee to lead the way. The transmission on the shuttle shifted gears as they headed out toward the Green Zone. Ryan instinctively reached down and touched the outside of his pants pocket, where he always carried his lucky silver dollar. Not feeling anything, he recalled that he had misplaced it.

Chapter Nineteen

MOLLY GREETED SARA AT THE side door after work. As Sara stood in the entrance, Molly titled her head in an attempt to see around her, and Sara knew that she was looking for Ryan.

"He had to go back to work, Molly girl." Sara set her purse down on the floor and petted Molly's head to comfort her. She knew that Molly missed Ryan. "I'm sorry, sweetie. I miss him too."

Sara picked up her purse and looped the straps around her forearm while she juggled her car keys in one hand and a stack of math tests in the other. She then set everything down and glanced at the answering machine, hoping that the little red light would be blinking to indicate that a message had been left while she was at work. The light on the machine only emitted a solid red glow.

She spent several hours searching the house for Ryan's silver dollar before making dinner for Molly and herself. Molly didn't seem to mind. In fact, she seemed to like their after-work hunting expedition. Their combined efforts, however, had managed to turn up merely one lost squeaky toy, about a dollar in loose change, an old shopping list, and a sock Sara was sure belonged to Russ.

Sara bent down and lifted up the bed skirt. As she peered under the bed from one side, Molly ran to the other side, poked her head under, and stared back at Sara. Undaunted, Sara then went downstairs to look between the cushions on the couch again. While it was a long shot, she even went outside and searched under the seats of the car. She found nothing under or between the seats. She then turned her attention to the bedroom closet, where Ryan's clothes hung. She searched all the pockets of his shirts, his jeans, and even those of his suit. As she was about to close the closet door, she noticed Ryan's boots sitting next to the door. She flipped the light on again and looked down into the boots; nothing. Exhausted, she sat on the edge of the bed as Molly looked up at her.

"Some detectives we are." Molly happily wagged her tail as Sara petted her. "Let's go fix us some dinner."

SARA HAD JUST FINISHED GRADING the math tests when she received Jane's daily phone call.

"Hello." Sara walked back to the dining room with the cordless phone cradled between her ear and shoulder and placed the red pen next to the stack of math tests.

"Sweetie, it's Jane. I gave Ryan's résumé to another client today."

"That's wonderful, thank you."

"That's not the best part. They want him in their office for an interview when he gets back from Iraq."

Sara could hear little Max barking in the background.

"Maxie, you come here to Mommy, and be a good boy."

Sara waited for the barking to stop before she said, "Jane, that's great news. I can't wait to tell Ryan."

"Did you find that coin yet?"

"Gone without a trace. I got an email from him yesterday and he said he dumped everything out of his briefcase and duffle bag again, and still nothing." Sara walked into the living room and sat down in her favorite chair. She reached around and pulled a quilt down over her lap as she listened to Jane.

"Sweetie, I misplaced my cow print bra once. I looked everywhere for that darn thing."

"A cow print bra?"

Jane ignored Sara's question and chatted nonstop. "Jakie took off work to meet the appliance repairman."

"A repairman? The repairman had your bra?" Sara did not comprehend. Molly strolled over and curled up next to Sara's chair.

"Don't you remember when I told you my drier was making that weird scraping noise? I would have paid good money to see my Jakie's face when that repairman pulled my 38D cow print bra from the back end of that drier!"

Sara burst into laughter as she pictured poor Jakie standing there red-faced with Jane's cow print bra in hand.

"That's it!"

"What's it?" Jane questioned.

"Jane, you're a genius! I gotta go!"

Sara quickly hung up on Jane and raced down the basement stairs. Molly barked and ran behind her. Sara stopped in front of the washer and drier.

"Please let it be here!" Sara prayed as she looked inside both the washer and drier. Unable to find anything, she was almost certain that Ryan's silver dollar had probably been left in his jeans pocket and ended up far from sight in the inner workings of one of the machines. She made a mental note to call the repairman tomorrow during recess and set up an appointment to have him come out to the house to look for the missing coin.

She rushed back upstairs to email Ryan and tell him the good news. But before she was able to compose an email to him, an email came through to her. Her eyes brightened when she noticed that it was from Ryan. The email featured an attached photo of Ryan and another man she could only assume was Al standing next to a large military tank.

Dear Sara,

I wish I could explain the way I feel. It is as if I am a stranger both to myself and this job I once loved so much. I think it is simply that I want to be home with you and Molly. When I sleep, I picture the next time I'll get to see you in my dreams. When I awake, my heart aches, because I know I still have weeks over here. I wish I could hold you in my arms; feel the touch of your skin next to mine.

Four more weeks left to go, and, trust me, I am counting them down.

You'll never guess what happened the other day. I was out on assignment, and as I got into a Humvee, I reached into one of the pockets on my flack vest and there was my silver dollar.

I better close for now. I have to be up very early in the morning, as we're going back out again on assignment.

Love,
Ryan

P.S. I had the rookie kid, Carl, snap a photo of Al and me for you.

Sara stared at the blinking cursor on the computer screen. Thank God he had found his lucky coin. Sara had never considered herself to be a superstitious person. Nevertheless, she breathed a sigh of relief knowing that Ryan had the coin with him. After she emailed him with the news that one of Jane's client's wanted him to come in for an interview once he returned home, she shut down her computer. She bundled up in a heavy jacket and went outside into the cold night air. Pulling the jacket tight around her, she sat down on the deck. This had become a nightly ritual since Ryan had been on assignment. She looked up at the night sky and smiled; just knowing that Ryan was seeing the same vast sky filled with the moon and stars made her feel closer to him. She closed her eyes and thought about what their life together would be like once he was safely back in her arms.

That night, as she drifted off to sleep, she thought of the day's events and the math papers she had graded after dinner. Suddenly, in her dreams, she pictured blood dripping onto the paper as she was correcting little Robert's math test.

"Ryan!" Sara screamed, waking herself and Molly.

She sat up in bed, shaking. She had not watched any news programs before going to bed; she had learned her lesson about that the first time Ryan was stationed over there. Why then was she having such a violent dream? It must have been something I ate, she thought to herself. Her mother always said spicy food could sometimes do this. That had to be what it was.

Chapter Twenty

RYAN CLICKED THE SEND button on his screen and watched the progress bar lengthen until his email went out into cyberspace, on its way to Sara's inbox back home. After closing the email program, he pressed the power button to shut off the laptop before closing the lid. He lay back on his bunk, closed his eyes, and began to picture Sara. And he swore, just for a second, that he could smell the soft scent of her perfume. He took a deep breath, pulling the imaginary scent into his lungs, and savored every second of it.

The sound of Al's snores resonating throughout the room brought him back to reality. Having had enough, he got up and quietly stepped outside their sleeping quarters. The moon and stars glowed brightly against the dark desert sky. Carl approached him, drying his hair with a towel, on his way back from the showers.

"Hey, Ryan, what's up?" It was a rhetorical question.

"Was there any water pressure tonight?" Ryan inquired

"Not much. I ended up using my bottled water to finish up."

"Welcome back to Iraq."

Carl smiled, and said, "It gets cold out here at night." He shivered as he turned and went inside.

Ryan looked up into the night sky and began to muse. There was one heaven above, and everyone experienced the same night sky, but in one region of the world there was peace, where people could live without fear, while in another there was unrest, hunger, and disease; but here, in this region, there was war and bloodshed. Why, he thought? He uttered a silent prayer, asking for guidance for the leaders of the world.

When he opened his eyes he watched as two young soldiers, who couldn't have been much older that eighteen, walked by.

"I miss you," he whispered under his breath. "Just a few more days and I'll be home." He took a deep breath, closed his eyes, and wished that he was already home, holding Sara in his arms.

THE CONVOY OF US SOLDIERS rolled to a dusty stop. Their objective this morning was to check several abandoned warehouses. As ordered, smoke bombs were deployed and colored smoke rose upward against the desert sky. The soldiers quickly and strategically made their way down the street behind the cloud of smoke, each darting from one area of the building to another. As one soldier found cover, another would approach. Inching their way in and around the buildings, they began the daunting task of going inside. Ryan and Al quickly climbed out of the Humvee and followed the platoon leader, Sergeant Hammer.

"Just another day in paradise," Ryan said, as he looked over at Al.

"Gee, now who has a rosy disposition?"

Instinctively, Ryan glanced up at the sun, noted its position in the sky, and then looked at his wristwatch. He jotted down the exact time, 7:05 a.m., on his notepad. Al started photographing the soldiers as they secured their positions.

Inside, they discovered maps and a cache of small arms and ammunition, and realized the real purpose of this building. Ryan jotted each and every detail in his journal.

Suddenly, the sound of rapid gunfire startled everyone in the building.

"Get down!" Hammer yelled to his men.

All of the men dove for the floor. The silence that followed was deafening as each man held his cover. Sergeant Hammer tilted his helmet up and looked around at the men located nearest to him. Without getting up, he pressed the button on the microphone attached to his radio, clicking it several times, which was a nonverbal signal to the team outside the building. The men close enough to hear lay on the dusty floor and waited for the clicks to be returned. The radio was silent. Sergeant Hammer pressed the button again. Still no response from the team outside.

A young private crawled over to the sergeant. “Sir, we’ve got two men down one floor up,” he said in a hushed tone.

“How bad are they?”

“One is dead. The other is still breathing, but bleeding badly, Sir.”

“Get the medic.”

The young private hesitated for a second.

The sergeant’s face hardened. “Find him now!”

“Sir, yes, Sir,” the young private said, crawling across the floor.

The medic checked a soldier who lay on the floor just inside the second floor entrance. Finding no pulse, he quickly maneuvered toward the figure of a man sitting on the floor, holding a body.

Al’s breathing was labored. His face was pale and riddled with pain. He kept trying to say something to Ryan but was unable to get the words out. The medic pulled Ryan away and began to apply a compression bandage to Al’s wounds. His body was already limp.

"Hang in there, buddy," Ryan managed to say, still shaken by the turmoil of the last few minutes. Al gasped his last breath. "Don't you do this." Ryan held onto one of Al's arms.

"He's gone," the medic said. "I'm sorry."

IT HAD BEEN THREE DAYS since Al's death. Ryan felt an indescribable numbness within his soul from that moment on. He kept repeating a silent ubiquitous question in his mind: Why? He and Al had both stepped into that room on the second floor of the warehouse with three soldiers that day. Ryan heard someone yell, "All clear!" Al started making a frame-by-frame photo journal of the room while Ryan gave an account of what he witnessed in words. Al was standing right next to him, on his right side. It wasn't the initial popping sound that Ryan recalled in the chain of events. What registered to him that something had gone terribly wrong was the spray of warm liquid that hit his face like rain. Oddly enough, the popping sounds seemed to come afterwards. He had immediately turned to his right where Al had been standing. But Al was gone. Suddenly he felt a tug at his pant leg. When he looked down he found Al lying on the floor, bleeding profusely.

From that point on, Ryan simply could not remember anything else that took place in that room on that day. When he got back to the base he remembered his boss, Steve, contacting him. He even recalled a brief email he sent to Sara, telling her that Al had been killed. He wanted to spare her, and even shelter her from what had happened. But he had to tell her that he would be escorting Al's body back to Kansas City, Missouri to his family, as soon as *The Post* and the military made the required arrangements. Following the funeral, he would be returning home to her.

All of the necessary paperwork was completed and in order four days after Al was killed. Ryan stood in a state of shock and denial as he watched Al's body being carried onto the plane. He even felt a sense of guilt as he stood there. He had heard accounts from surviving soldiers who, many times, suffered from what was known as survivor's guilt. He wondered if that could be the reason he felt the way he did.

The nudging of an unknown soldier made Ryan move up the ramp robotically as he boarded the military transport plane. Nothing he or anyone did could ease the grief and shock of losing his best friend. He slumped down in one of the webbed seats and buckled himself in for the flight. He had made this trip to Kuwait City many times before heading back to the United States. However, this trip was different. Al no longer sat next to him. In fact, no one occupied the seat to Ryan's left where Al always sat. The empty seat, which Ryan gazed at several times during the flight, made everything seem surreal to him. Without knowing why or caring what anyone thought, he reached over and buckled the belt in the empty seat. Then he leaned back and wiped a tear from his eye.

SARA SAT STUNNED, WIPING the tears from her eyes. She read Ryan's email over and over again, as if rereading the message would somehow change the outcome of events. While she sat staring in disbelief at the blinking cursor on the computer screen, she felt grateful that Ryan had not been hurt. Nevertheless, she was able to read between the lines of his short, fragmented message, and sensed the pain he must be feeling. While his return date to Boston was still uncertain, she was relieved to know that he would be leaving Iraq soon and heading back to the United States.

Sara anxiously awaited Ryan's homecoming. Several days after she had last heard from him, she felt ill at school. She thought that maybe she was coming down with something. After all, three of her students were out sick. She tried to put it out of her mind, knowing that stress might also be the cause.

As soon as school was over, Sara went straight home and made herself a warm bowl of soup. She left the stack of mail on the foyer table untouched and decided to curl up with a book in her favorite chair instead. She heard the phone ring a few minutes later, so she got up to check the caller ID. It was Ryan's cell phone number.

Sara caught the call on the third ring, and said, "Hello." She waited for Ryan's voice, but was greeted only with silence.

"Hello," she repeated before hearing the line go dead.

"Cell phones," she muttered to herself. She dialed his number back, but all she heard was Ryan's recorded voice.

After sitting back down, she found her place in the book and resumed reading. Just then, Molly stood up suddenly, ran over to the loveseat against the far wall, and barked. Startled, Sara looked up at Molly as she stood in front of the blue loveseat. Molly's head was tilted back and she was looking up as she continued to bark.

"Molly, you goof," Sara said, "you're barking at a loveseat."

Molly slowly walked back to Sara and lay back down at her feet. Every few minutes, however, she would raise her head and glance over at the loveseat.

"B-r-r-r," Sara said, shivering. Feeling a sudden chill, she reached for a quilt on the back of the chair and wrapped it around herself. While she did not feel like she was coming down with the flu, or even a cold, she simply did not feel like herself.

STEVE STOOD UP AS Lisa Green came into his office. He walked over to the door and closed it, then he walked around his desk and took his seat again.

"Here is the file you requested." Lisa carefully placed the folder on his desk and pulled up a chair.

After opening the manila folder, Steve thumbed through several papers. Lisa noticed that he was having difficulty, so she reached over and pulled the first paper from the file.

"I believe this is what you're looking for," she said, handing the paper to him. She noticed his hand was trembling as he took it from her.

"Thank you, Lisa," he said, looking up at her. "I'll take it from here."

Chapter Twenty-One

MRS. KELLY SAT HUNCHED over the kitchen table, staring at the word puzzle in the newspaper. It was a difficult one today; even she would have to admit it. But Gladys Kelly was no amateur. She was not going to allow this puzzle to go unsolved and simply end up in the recycling bin without each row being filled in. Like a sleuth, she worked diligently for hours, figuring out each clue.

It was shortly before 5:00 p.m. Daylight was beginning to fade, giving way to another brisk New England evening, when she heard a scream. Mrs. Kelly knew that this wasn't the joyful scream of a neighborhood child at play. No, this was a piercing scream made by someone in pain. Without concern for herself, she jumped up from the kitchen chair so fast that she almost knocked it over. She grabbed the baseball bat that she kept behind the kitchen door and ran outside. While standing on her back step, she heard the screams again. This time she could hear them clearly. They were coming from the direction of Sara's house.

She scurried over to the side door, knowing that

Sara sometimes left it unlocked—even though she had told her that she shouldn't. When she entered the house, she found Sara lying on the kitchen floor, curled up in a fetal position and sobbing uncontrollably.

"Where is he?" Gladys demanded, as she pivoted around, looking in every direction.

Molly whined and paced around Sara frantically. She had never seen Sara behave like this before.

"He's gone." Sara cried

"Who?" Gladys asked.

"He's gone," Sara cried, over and over again.

"Which way did he go? I'm callin' the cops!" Gladys never let her guard down, nor did she lower the baseball bat from her shoulder.

The ringing of the telephone caused Gladys to jump. She spun around and snatched up the handset. "Hello, who is this?" Gladys demanded.

"Who is this?" Jane asked, taken aback by the stranger who had answered Sara's phone.

"Gladys Kelly."

Eventually, Sara was able to take the phone from Mrs. Kelly. "No survivors." She sobbed uncontrollably into the phone.

"Sweetie, what are you talking about?" Jane asked, confused.

"No survivors . . . were found. He's gone!" Sara could only manage to say a word or two before she laid the phone on the floor.

"Gladys!" Jane screamed into the phone loud enough for Mrs. Kelly to hear, and she picked up the receiver. "Gladys, stay with her until I can get there."

After Jane arrived, it took several minutes for Sara to gather enough strength to tell Jane that Ryan had been killed in a plane crash.

A WEEK AFTER RYAN'S DEATH, Sara went back to work, and Jane, who had been staying with her, went home to Jakie. Even Jane believed it was best for her to try and live life the way she did before Ryan was killed, even if it was only a semblance of that life. Jane stopped by each evening to sit and visit with Sara. During one of these visits, Molly began her usual barking at the loveseat.

"I'm going to have to make a vet appointment for her." Sara looked over at Molly as she wagged her tail and barked at the loveseat.

"How long has this been going on?" Jane asked, concerned.

Sara thought for a moment. "It started the night that Ryan's plane went down."

"When you and Ryan were here together, where did you both usually sit?"

"The loveseat." Sara did not understand what

this had to do with Molly's barking at thin air.

Jane said, "She sees Ryan when he visits you."

"She sees . . . ?" Sara stopped mid-sentence, thinking about what Jane had just said. She looked over at the loveseat and then back at Jane, her face in total confusion.

"Sweetie," Jane said, "pets have a keen sense, unlike us humans do. Also, they aren't encumbered by what they should or should not believe in."

Sara quickly changed the subject. "So I bet Max is happy to have you back home."

Jane started chatting away about Max. But Sara found it hard to focus, as her mind wandered in and out of the conversation. The best she could do these days was simply smile and nod, and this is what she did while Jane talked.

Less than two weeks after Ryan's death, Sara was going through her mail when she pulled a postcard from the stack. She sat down, her hands trembling, and turned the card over to read it.

Dear Sara,

I just had a few minutes to write and wanted to tell you how much you are loved and missed. I close my eyes and see you reaching out to me and it feels like heaven. If only my arms could reach that far.

Love,
Ryan

Sara sat staring at the postcard. It all felt strange as she reread his words. She jumped at the sound of the ringing doorbell. Molly ran to the front door ahead of her. Sara walked to the door, opened it a crack, and found a man standing on her doorstep holding a dozen red roses.

"Yes?" Sara said.

"I have a delivery for Ms. Sara Ketcham."

Sara noticed the one long stemmed rose with the dog biscuit attached.

"No!" She screamed, and then broke down crying. "I don't need flowers, I need him!"

"But . . . I . . ." The young man was at a loss for words, given Sara's reaction.

"Take them back! They can't be from him!" Sara watched the young man turn around and walk toward the delivery van. "No. No. Wait. I'm sorry."

Sara opened the door wide and motioned him to bring them in. The young man was quick about bringing the flowers in and setting them on the foyer table, and he left before she had a chance to change her mind. Sara handed the biscuit to Molly and sat staring at the vase of roses. *How could this be happening? Could Ryan's boss have given me the wrong information?* She was still on the couch holding the postcard with trembling hands when Jane arrived.

"Sweetie, what is it?" Jane looked around and noticed the roses.

"They're from Ryan." Sara held out the postcard. "So is this."

Jane quickly read the card. Before she did anything else, she inspected the envelope that accompanied the roses. After noting the florist's name, she went into the kitchen with the envelope in hand and dialed the number printed on it. Sara sat with Molly at her feet, never moving; she just stared at the flowers. Jane returned a few minutes later.

"Sara, sweetie, Ryan had paid in advance to have the flowers delivered every two weeks. I can just imagine how this makes you feel." Jane waited until Sara finally stopped staring at the roses and looked up at her. "As for the postcard, I simply cannot make out the postmark."

"I want it to be from him. I want this to all be a big mistake." Sara broke down crying and Jane had to hold her. "I want him to come home and walk through that door."

"Sweetie, they are from him, but he's not coming back. I'm so sorry."

"I called his cell phone today." Fresh tears spilled onto her cheeks.

"You what?" Jane pulled a tissue out of the box on the coffee table and handed it to her. "Oh, sweetie, you didn't."

Sara's lips quivered "I guess they haven't disconnected it yet. I just wanted to hear his voice again."

For the next few weeks, postcards and letters continued to come to the house, along with another vase of roses. Sometimes it was simply easier for her to envision him still being over there; still at work; still alive. Other days, the letters and postcards brought tears to her eyes.

One Saturday morning, seven weeks to the day that Ryan was killed—and while Sara was still asleep—the doorbell rang. Sara woke up at the sound of Molly barking and frantically scratching at the front door. She slipped on her bathrobe and tied it as she went down the stairs. After opening the door a crack, she squinted and looked out into the bright sunlight. A man had just stepped off the front step and was heading toward a car parked in the driveway.

Sara called after him. "Yes, can I help you?"

The young man turned and, for a split-second, something about him reminded her of Ryan. She thought, maybe it's the well-tanned face, or is it?

"Are you Sara Ketcham?" the man inquired.

"Yes."

The man nervously shifted his weight from one leg to the other. "My name is Carl . . . Carl Miller. I worked with Spence."

Sara stood motionless, holding onto the open door. "Spence?"

"Ryan Spencer." Carl hesitated for a moment, and then extended his hand to her. In the palm of his hand was the silver Peace Dollar Ryan had always carried.

"Where did you get this!" Sara's voice cracked with emotion. "He always carried it with him!" Her eyes filled with tears as she took the coin into her hand.

"I'm . . . sorry. Maybe I shouldn't have come. I . . . just thought you would want it."

Sara opened the front door and stepped aside. Unable to speak, she motioned for Carl to come in and have a seat in the living room.

"Ms. Ketcham–"

Sara interrupted. "Please, call me Sara."

"Sara, the night before Ryan left camp, he told me his flack vest was better than the one I had." Carl hesitated a moment. He gazed at Sara as she dabbed the tears from her eyes while looking at the coin in her hand. "The day I heard about Ryan's plane going down, I found his coin in the pocket of the vest he gave me."

Sara sat in silence, attempting to absorb what

Carl was telling her. She asked, “How on earth did you find me?”

Carl reached into his jacket pocket and handed her an unopened letter she had sent to Ryan. “This came after he left. I knew your name was Sara and it was on the return address.” Carl stood and handed the letter to Sara. “I should be going.” He walked toward the door and turned back. “Sara, I’m sorry about Ryan. He was a good friend.”

IT WAS THE STRESS, SHE told herself, that was causing her to feel rundown and tired. Nevertheless, she made an appointment with her doctor. The chill in the exam room sent shivers down her spine. Sara sat on the examination table with her bare legs dangling, and clothed only in a hospital gown. She felt so alone as she waited for her doctor to return.

It took almost a week for the news to truly sink in. One evening, Jane stopped by the house to check on Sara. They sat and made small talk with each other until Sara looked over at Jane.

“I’m pregnant.”

Epilogue

Five Years Later

THE OCEAN SWIRLED BEFORE her as waves rolled up onto the shore and receded back out to sea again. A light breeze lifted her dark brown hair as she sat next to the water's edge. There was a smile on her lips as she stared out across the water. Sara loved being here at Brant Rock, close to the ocean, and far away from the city. She had always found peace beside the water. After slipping off her sandals, she felt the moist sand between her toes, and she tasted a hint of salt on her lips.

Sara turned and watched her daughter, Emma, playing with Molly in the sand. Emma had spent the better part of the morning working on a sandcastle, with Molly leaving her side only long enough to chase a seagull into flight. She watched as Emma's little hands molded a protective wall around the castle.

"There," Emma said. "The wall will protect our castle, Molly."

Molly stood up and wagged her tail, in obvious acceptance of Emma's observation. Sara smiled, wishing life could only be that simple, and opened her journal to a blank page.

Dear Ryan,

It's been five years since you have been gone. While I feel your presence each and every day beside me, I still grieve within me for what we could have had. I miss your gentle touch, the sound of your voice, and the way you used to hold me at night. There are so many things I miss about you; one would have thought we were together for a lifetime. I think Jane is right, that we knew each other long before we met in this lifetime. Funny, when I think back to the very first day our eyes met at the inn, there was just something about you, which I cannot explain. Sweetheart, you taught me to trust and love again. For that I will be eternally grateful. I was more loved by you in that short time than most women are in a lifetime. In fact, I still feel your love.

I still wear the beautiful ring you picked out for me. I plan to give it to Emma one day, when she is old enough and can appreciate something so sentimental.

Love,
Sara

Sara turned the page and closed her journal. She looked up and watched Emma inspecting her work. Emma turned and noticed that Sara was watching her. She ran back to Sara's side along with Molly.

Emma asked, "Are you writing Daddy another letter?"

"Yes, sweetheart. I am."

"Mommy, tell me again about Daddy and the postcards, p-l-e-a-s-e!"

Sara looked at her daughter and smiled. "You know what?"

"What?" Emma smiled and giggled.

Sara reached over and touched little Emma's cheek. "You have your Daddy's dimples. Right there." Sara pointed to her dimples.

Emma shrieked with joy. "I do?"

"You most certainly do."

"Mommy, p-l-e-a-s-e tell the story again."

"You want to hear about the postcards?"

"Yes!" Emma sat, waiting for her mother to tell her the story.

"Let's see. . . . Almost every other day, for about five weeks, after Daddy's plane went down—"

Emma shook her head and interrupted, telling Sara, "I don't like that part, Mommy."

"You know what, sweetheart? Neither do I," Sara said, deep in thought. "But life is about taking the bad with the good, and mixing it all together."

Emma watched intently as Sara's hand moved about, stirring the imaginary mixture together.

Sara continued: "And making something wonderful out of it . . . like you."

Emma giggled again.

"The postcards first started about a week or so. . . ." Sara's eyes became watery as she remembered the arrival of the first few postcards. "You know what?" Sara said, as she leaned over and looked at Emma.

"What?" Emma's eyes widened with excitement.

"I like to think the postcards came from heaven."

"Me too, Mommy!"

About the Author

TIMOTHY GLASS was born in Pennsylvania, but he moved to the southwest with his family as a child. Tim graduated from the University of New Mexico. He spent some time in New England before moving back to Albuquerque, New Mexico, where he now resides. More than 300 of his nonfiction articles have been published nationally and internationally. The author of *Just This Side of Heaven*, he is currently working on several writing projects, including the popular *Sleepytown Beagles* series. A staff writer for a global monthly newsletter put out by OurDogHouse.com, Tim is also working on a nonfiction book, *Until the End of Time*, and an animated screenplay, *Hero*. He is a member of the Author's Guild of America, Author's League of America, and a past member of IEEE Computer Society. Tim enjoys the company of his wife, Cathy, and his tri-colored beagles, as well as hiking, weight training, and woodworking.

The inspiration for this book came from the many years Tim worked as a journalist. He was offered an assignment in the Middle East as an embedded reporter. After initially accepting, he later turned it down for personal reasons. It has always been a missing link in his journalistic career—not accepting the assignment—and he deeply regrets this decision.

www.ingramcontent.com/pod-product-compliance
Lightning Source LLC
Chambersburg PA
CBHW030334310726
48979CB00001B/32
* 9 7 8 0 9 9 8 4 1 2 1 5 3 *